I0685770

Space Traipse:

Hold My Beer

Season Four

Karina L. Fabian

LASER COW
PRESS

Laser Cow Press

Merritt Island, FL

Laser Cow Press, LLC
Merritt Island, FL
www.fabianspace.com

Book Layout ©2017 BookDesignTemplates.com
Cover Art by Dawn Grimes
Logo by Ann Lewis

Space Traipse: Hold My Beer, Season 4/ Karina Fabian.—1st ed.

ISBN   978-1-7334471-9-5

To William Shatner, and all the shirts he ripped in the making of Star Trek

And to Robert Picardo – Doc Sorcha may not agree about striving to be human, but that doesn't mean I loved your character any less!

Space: By Keptar, there's a lot of it. And it's chock-full of stuff to do and people to meet. These are the adventures of the HMB Impulsive. Its mission: to explore worlds, to seek out anomalies, and to boldly do what no one else has the guts to do! And you know that we're the ship to do it.

Don't believe me? Hold my beer!

Contents

A Note on Vocabulary: Words evolve, especially when influenced by other cultures. This is true in the Space Traipse universe, too. In addition to some new alien words, there are some words—English and foreign—that are misspelled. This is deliberate. I also decided not to italicize them, since they are part of the ST: HMB vernacular.   Italics   are   for   emphasis.

Love is Many Stars

Captain's Log, Intergalactic Date 676952.89

After a couple of exceedingly difficult missions, we're finally getting a break—literally and figuratively. The Impulsive will dock at Organa Station, Europa, for a week of R&R while the ship is thoroughly scoured to remove any sign of the cybervirus. We're also hosting the team that created the janbots as they install better security features. Even so, I think we're all ready for some time off and some good news.

In other good news, Ensign Ellie Doall received her promotion to Lieutenant. 'Bout time the paperwork got processed. Sometimes, I think HuFleet just delays promotions, so we have at least one super-competent ensign on the bridge. Now, with Ensign Gel showing his awesomeness, we can let Ellie get the recognition she so richly deserves. Ensign Leslie Straus has also been promoted, and well deserved, there, too.

We held the ceremony just before docking. That way, they can celebrate with their friends on the station instead of having a party on the ship. No one is interested in singing and dancing on this ship until it's been scoured.

Because of the potential for infecting the station with the cybervirus, the Impulsive was connected to the starbase only by a simple mechanical docking tube. The first rotation of shore-leave crewmen queued patiently in the corridor, while Ensign Gel O'Tin oozed along the line, reciting the same litany:

"Leave all computers and computerized equipment on the Impulsive. That includes communicators and credit chips. You'll use fingerprints to accrue tabs on Organa. If you are carrying any liquids, drink them now.

"When you get to the airlock, place your feet on the yellow footprints, put your arms up, and wait until told to step forward. Do not shake your hips. Do not shimmy. Anyone looking like they are dancing, even in sarcasm, will be stunned for the good of the station. Headaches save lives!"

"Headaches save lives!" responded some of the crew. After being forced to live in a musical for the past few days, anyone making a joke about dancing deserved to be shot. Most, however, ignored Gel, talking excitedly about plans.

Lieutenant Ellie Doall, Lieutenant Leslie Straus, Lieutenant Misha Rosien, and several of their female friends stood in a tight knot, giggling over their plans.

"And we are going to dance," Leslie said, "actual real dancing. Unscripted, with real men who are not interested in taking our minds."

"Agreed!" Ellie said. She'd had enough of suitors—biological or cybernetic—wanting her mind.

The girls high-fived, an ancient human ritual that managed to survive even into this century, because if handshakes can survive that long (even through COVID-19), why not the joyful hand-slap? Efforts to introduce the gesture to other species have mostly failed, however. The fragile mandibles of the Snoephlak species snapped on impact (#32 of Loreli's First Contacts Gone FUBAR lecture). Alternately, high-fiving a member of the paranoid species Hoodat usually resulted in a palmful of needles, the Hoodat's natural defense. The Logics, of course, found the physical display of emotion as embarrassing as public snogging. If they would ever admit embarrassment, that is.

Most species just found it weird.

Gel, having been among humans most of his adult life, was used to the gesture and appreciated its meaning. He paused in his pacing the line to address the group. "Just do me a favor and don't get into too much trouble? The LT put me in charge tonight, and I don't want to have to bail anyone out."

Leslie laughed. "No promises. Right, Misha?"

Her friend shrugged. She looked at Gel only long enough to give him a quick, awkward smile.

Gel ignored her discomfort. He congratulated Ellie and Leslie once more before starting further down the line, reciting his speech.

"Headaches save lives!" Leslie shouted, then turned to Misha. "Meesh, he's really sorry. How long are you going to be mad?"

"So where's Lieutenant LaFuentes going tonight?" Misha asked. She stepped forward as the line moved, and the knot of friends moved with her.

Leslie sighed, accepting the change in subject. "He got a comms from one of his babymamas. Raquella, I think. She and their daughter, Marisol, are on the station. I guess there's a beauty pageant going on, and she's in it. He's already on the station. He seemed pretty confused by it all."

There were nods all around. How anyone born and bred on the Genship The Hood could aspire to, much less compete in, a pageant was difficult to take in.

"And no jokes about her 'killing the competition,'" Leslie warned as they made it to the airlock. "Tank made one, and he's in his quarters, sleeping off a stun."

At the virus detector, Minion LeRoy Jenkins smiled at the ladies. "I'm just glad he said it first," he told them. "One at a time, please. Feet on the footprints, hands up, don't move..."

As they headed down the docking tube, they passed a young woman going the other way. Dressed in what they assumed were the latest fashions, she combined grace with delight, as if traversing the docking tube were a great honor. She beamed and waved at the knot of ladies as they passed by. In fact, she beamed and waved at everyone.

"Who's that?" Ellie asked.

Captain's Log, Continued

Shore leave and the resulting down time will also give the crew some time to truly process the loss of Lieutenant Loreli, our xenologist and Ship's Sexy. Some are having a harder time than others—in particular, Teleporter Chief Dour. Since the accident, he's been teleporting himself around the ship. We originally thought that he was testing the equipment, but after he accidentally teleported into Lieutenant Doall's shower while she was in it, we realized he has a problem.

Doctor Sorcha said 'tepping,' is a mental illness sometimes found in teleporter experts, a kind of self-harm without the actual harm. This is not the first time Chief Dour's been stricken, and we are concerned. He is in Sickbay under observation but has refused to talk. Fortunately, there's someone on the station who might be able to help.

"Captain," Minion Jenkins said, "May I introduce to you Miss Gloria Joy Dour."

Captain Jebediah Tiberius smiled welcomingly at the graceful, vivacious woman who walked into his ready room on the arm of Minion Jenkins, but only because years of practice enabled him to keep his surprise from showing on his face. This was Chief Dour's sister?

It wasn't just that she was beautiful—Dolfrick himself was attractive enough for his gender—but more that she was conspicuously so. Jeb knew the type growing up in Texas. Gloria Joy Dour worked at being the kind of beauty that turned heads without spoiling hearts, that made female-attracted beings want to put her on a pedestal while making those not so romantically inclined just want to be besties. Minion Jenkins' happy ease around her suggested she was also as gracious as she was lovely.

She gave LeRoy a last wave as he walked out, then turned her full attention to the Captain, giving him her hand. "Such a fine young man, a credit to your ship. I can see why Dolfrick was so pleased about this assignment. But I'm sure you know how wonderful your ship is, and I think you're not the kind of man who wants to bandy about with small talk. So please, what's happened to my brother? I must admit, I'm surprised not to see your doctor here, too."

"Dr. Sorcha is unable to leave Sickbay," Jeb started but paused as Gloria Joy went pale and sank into a seat.

"Is Dolfrick that bad?" she asked.

"No, no!" He took the seat beside her and clasped her hands in his reassuringly. "Our doctor is the emergency medical photonic technician. She can't leave the holoemitters on Sickbay. Your brother is confined to Sickbay for his own good and the peace of mind of the crew, but he's… erm…"

"Sulking?" Her tone reflected annoyance and endearment.

Jeb shrugged and nodded. Briefly, he explained to her how Loreli died in a teleporter accident, leaving out all the classified details. Most people in the Union did not know that the Cybers were behind the bizarre reprogramming of the replicators or the sudden dissolution— almost literally—of the planet Filedise from which nearly all replicator patterns come.

Certainly, they did not need to know that Filedise had in fact been hired by the Cybers to create a program unlocking the secret of human success as a race—a quality they called kuricrearrogance.

Yep, Jeb left almost all of that out, and if you are confused, then may I suggest reading *Space Traipse: Hold My Beer, Season 3* or finding Episode 7 on my blog? It's worth your time, promise.

For the rest of you, let's move on.

"It's not often we lose a crewman on this ship, and even more rare that we lose a protag—a prominent member like Lieutenant Loreli. It's hit all of us hard, but..."

"...but Dolfy runs the teleporters. I think I understand. May I see him now?"

"Of course." They rose, and she took his arm just as she had taken LeRoy's.

As they walked to Sickbay, she turned the conversation to his job and dreams. Jeb found himself just as charmed as his security minion had been.

Dr. Sorcha met them at the door of Sickbay. Unlike many Sickbays, there is a small alcove between the corridors and the patient beds. I mean, seriously, who wants to walk into Sickbay because of the sniffles and interrupt someone undergoing surgery or lying in bed after having been mauled on a disastrous away mission to a seemingly ideal Class M planet whose one indigent predator species has a thing against red shirts? Hence, the alcove, which has a waiting room, a doctor's office, and a ready supply of tissue.

Gloria Joy gasped as she took in the hologram. "My goodness! You're gorgeous!"

The doctor bowed her head in acknowledgment. "Appearances are important for my secondary function as Ship's Sexy. I shall pass your compliments to our Chief Engineer and Ops Officer, who programmed me. Has the Captain briefed you on your brother's situation?"

"Yes. I didn't want too many details. I'd rather Dolfrick tell me himself. They say that opening up is the best treatment, and it's harder if I go in with preconceived notions."

Dr. Sorcha's expression changed to one of admiration. "I agree. He has been in a catatonic-like state for several hours. Have you had psychiatric training?"

"Oh, only for my job, which involves quite a bit of consoling people, let me tell you. But I also know my brother. I do hope you won't mind if I'm not 'textbook' in my approach."

"I am interested only in results," Dr. Sorcha said. "I am here to advise, but I won't interfere. Are you ready to see him?"

At her assent, the doors opened.

Teleporter Chief Dolfrick Dour lay on a bed at the far end of the room, unmoving. He wore his black ceremonial robes. His arms were crossed over his chest, as if in anticipation of the coffin, and he stared unblinkingly at the ceiling.

"Dolfin!" Gloria Joy cried, and hurried to him, making rapid squeaky noises.

The Goth teleporter chief turned his head and sat up. "What? How... Why?"

Seeing the captain's surprised blink, Dr. Sorcha said, "I did say, 'catatonic-like.'"

With a final skip, Gloria stopped in front of him and hugged him. "It's me! Gloria Joy, silly. And I boarded through the airlock. I'm still your pure, undefiled big sister." She held out her hand as if expecting him to examine it for any signs that she'd been 'defiled' by a teleporter.

Despite his confusion, he cradled her slender arm in both of his hands and peered at her skin.

"As for why, to see you! I'm on the station with a few of the Miss Universe finalists to do a variety show for the staff, and I heard you were feeling even more gloomy-doomy than normal, so I dropped everything to come turn your frown upside down. I'm starving! Why don't we go to the cafeteria or whatever you call it, and get some lunch, and you can tell me all about it?"

Dolfrick glowered at her as if a storm were brewing and his frown was the only umbrella he'd get. He let her arm drop. "*Little* sister, and I have no intention of taking you anywhere public, much less our mess so you can consume half a salad."

She tsked. "I'm not seventeen anymore, Dolfin. I eat the whole salad, with protein."

"Congratulations on your newfound decadence."

"And you can't get rid of me that easily. In fact, your captain said I can stay as long as I want. Didn't you, Captain Jeb?"

"Captain Jeb" found himself grinning. He had three younger sisters, and Keptar's crack if

Gloria Joy didn't sound like the youngest. Now he understood why his dad often hid a grin. "In fact, I have."

"I cannot be ordered to talk to you." Dour's pronouncement came like a death knell, and following that, he again reclined, resting his hands over his chest.

After a moment, Gloria Joy sighed and started pulling at his robes.

"What are you doing?" he snarled.

"Well, if you are going to lay in state, you ought to at least do it without wrinkles. We wouldn't want *your mistress* to think you were getting sloppy."

His jaw worked a moment, then he spat out, "Thank you."

She continued fussing a few moments longer, anyway, then wiped her hands. "Much better. Now, I'm going to get myself a Flausian salad with extra kirfbird, and then I'll catch you up on everything you've missed. Uh, Doctor, where...?"

Dr. Sorcha had already materialized her order in a replicator and brought it to her, along with a chair and one of those funny wheeled tables that fit over the bed and whose design has been so useful in hospitals that no one has significantly changed it in centuries.

Gloria Joy clapped her hands in delight. She sat primly and stabbed at the leaves with a fork, speaking cheerily between bites. "So, let's see. I think I mentioned we're here for a variety show, right? This year, part of the competition is to take every contestant on the road for a few weeks to entertain in different venues. It was my idea, actually. It's like I always said, 'the most important part of being Miss Universe is in the wide range of beings whose lives you touch...'"

He sighed.

* * *

Back on the starbase, Ellie and Company were also enjoying a wide range of beings, having eaten, drank, and flirted at several of the establishments on the entertainment ring. Around midnight, most of the party returned to the ship to sleep or sober up before their shift.

"I should go, too. I have that meeting tomorrow," Ellie said, but for once, her heart wasn't aligned with her sense of duty. The people responsible for programming the janbots were coming to get briefed and diagnose the security vulnerabilities that let the Cybers in. For a few hours, she'd all but forgotten about how Janbot had somehow developed feelings for her and tried to trap her mind in a weird cybernetic universe.

Leslie, of course, picked up on her reluctance. "Oh, come on. It's a meeting. Sisco is giving the briefing. You're just there to answer questions about your experience. How much prep do you need for that?"

"True, but…"

Misha took her arm. "Please? We're having so much fun, and I'm not tired yet, and I want to go back to The Protector and do more line dancing. I was just getting the hang of The Thermian!" She let go to demonstrate, marching along, hands rising with her knees, as she badly sang a song they'd only learned a couple of hours ago. She managed to stay coordinated until the time came to change direction, at which point, she stumbled into Ellie. She latched onto her both to support herself and to plead. "Please? We'll have you home by 0200."

Ellie laughed as she helped her upright. "Okay! A couple more hours can't hurt."

Misha squealed with joy, and the three of them returned to their favorite spot of the evening—both for the music and the selection of potential dance partners. They took a table near enough to the floor to signal their interest in dancing but far enough that they could still talk. Leslie ordered them three Digitizers. They slammed them down quickly. Ellie gasped as the liquid fire struck her insides, making them feel like they'd been turned inside out and exploded.

Misha sputtered as she giggled.

Leslie may as well have chugged water. "All right. Now that it's just the three of us, what the hell was this security report I saw about Dour materializing in your sonic shower?"

"Dour in your shower?" Misha said. "What did you do?"

"I screamed, of course!" Ellie said, making Leslie bark out a laugh that drew looks from other tables. She waved at them, still laughing.

Misha, however, had lost her giggles. "I didn't think Dour was like that."

"He's not, and that's what was so disturbing. I mean, he didn't even look at me. He just stared at the drain and said, 'The perfect metaphor,' and then he dematerialized."

Leslie smacked the table as if the motion would help her catch her breath. "'The perfect metaphor'? Now that is exactly like Dour. Oh, wow. I wonder if he's going to write a depressing poem about it. *Before me, she stood/Naked in her fury/Out of my shower*!"

"*As suds flowed to their oblivion,*" Ellie concluded, then snickered herself. The Digitizer must have caught up with her.

"Guys!" Misha protested.

"Come on. It's funny. Only Dour could be so oblivious as to ignore a naked woman, especially one as gorgeous as Ellie."

"Aw, thanks!" Ellie clasped her hands to her chest to contain the swell of love and happiness she felt at the compliment. Or maybe it was the alcohol.

"It's true, and you know it." Leslie patted her shoulder, then seeing Misha's incredulous look, turned serious. "Weird things happen in space, Meesh. Like with you and Gel. He's still upset about it, you know. He never meant to go creepy ooze monster on you. The *blook* Vis drugged him silly."

Misha bit her lip apprehensively, clearly unsure what to say next. Ellie reached out to grasp her arm. "It's okay. We're friends here. No judgement. Right, Leslie?"

"What we discuss here stays between us three girls," Leslie promised.

"We just hate seeing you two like this," Ellie added.

While Misha decides what to say next, let's do a quick catchup for those unfortunates who have not read "Amock Time" in *Space Traipse: Hold My Beer, Season 2.*

When Gel became an ensign, the ruling genetic authority on his planet decided it was time for him to come home and fulfill his procreative responsibilities. To ensure he did so, they slipped him a hormonal subpoena. (Yes, legally induced pon farr. You're welcome.) However, his assigned mate, Vis Koos, manipulated the chemicals in the said subpoena to make him lose his self-control, hoping he'd make a fool of himself in front of everyone so she could reject him. If you want to know how things ended, go read the story. (Hint: Gel made the Impulsive proud.) What you *do* need to know right now is that Misha had gone to talk to him while he was out of his right mind, and he tried to envelop her. Things have been tense between them since.

It's a very unfunny part of an otherwise humorous parody of ST:TOS's "Amok Time," which is why we're addressing it more now.

As the narrator provided backstory and Ellie squeezed Misha's arm reassuringly, Leslie was giving the room a casual surveillance. Misha didn't notice, and Ellie wasn't insulted. She knew it was a habit ingrained in her friend after years on the Impulsive under Lieutenant LaFuentes's tutelage. When they first came in, Leslie had noted the exits, cataloged the potential weapons (bottles, chairs, a Raisian's stunner—about as effective as watered-down mace would be on humans), and calculated the distance to the bar. Ellie guessed she was reevaluating the threat level—or maybe the party potential.

Leslie patted Misha's hand, but with a subtle gesture directed Ellie's gaze to a trio of guys a couple of tables away, also engrossed in conversation with one morose member. Nice looking, the lot of them.

Misha finally said, "He apologized, and I know he feels awful. It's just... Since it happened, every time I see him, I feel goo oozing up my legs..."

"No, I get it," Leslie said. "I have to train with him—or more to the point, against him. Everyone in Security has to. After the first couple of sparring sessions, I had to take a long shower. I think all of us did. If it helps any, I don't think he's always comfortable dealing with solids, either."

Misha paused, considering. "That kind of does. And really, he wasn't malicious or anything, just confused. I do forgive him. Problem is, even though I'm getting past the actual incident, things are so weird between us, I don't know how to act. Seriously, where in HuFleet do they teach you how to handle it when one of your crewmates starts acting like carnivorous slime?"

"I think the LT is working on it," Leslie said. She caught the attention of the waitress, an easy thing to do since the waitress was a Pelotann and had three faces in her round head, and ordered three more drinks.

"You're not going to transfer, are you?" Ellie asked. "It's just, there's a rumor..."

"A pool, you mean," Misha said. "I heard. I thought about it, but let's face it—our job is to explore the galaxy, and I'm an exobotanist. There's a good chance I may one day get attacked by sapient slime. First time might as well be a friend."

The waitress set three more glasses on the table, so they toasted to friendly slime and first times.

Leslie must have ordered something different, Ellie thought, because it just burned instead of reversing the polarity of her innards. Or maybe she was just getting inured. She was starting to feel pleasantly lightheaded, so when the three guys introduced themselves and asked to join them, she was glad to make room. She turned to give one a perky, winning smile, and looked straight into the most beautiful, soulful eyes she'd ever seen.

"I'm Todd," he said. His accent tickled her ears. His shy smile held a hint of sadness. She had the crazy urge to kiss it away.

"Oh." The word came out as a small gasp. Her body felt like goo, and she totally wanted to ooze herself all over him. She mentally strangled the thought and the metaphor as a bad idea and held out her hand instead. "Ellie." Despite the confidence that clichés say comes with alcohol and promotions, she spoke at half her usual volume.

"It's a pleasure to meet you, Awlie."

"Yes," she agreed, and didn't bother to modify her statement. She knew immediately that he understood her.

* * *

Gel enjoyed his first night managing security on his own. Before the LT had commandeered him for the Impulsive, he'd served station security on Starbase 119/Organa Station, mostly on bouncer duty. Handling station security on the starship side was much easier. Back then, he'd dealt with up to 15 fights a night, earning the wrath of the combatants for interfering and the ire of the bartenders for never responding fast enough. Tonight, he'd bailed out two drunk engineers who got into a fight with a couple of Raisians who called the Impulsive names before realizing their stun guns weren't going to save them from its crew. That, and a crowd of crewmen who had drunk a few too many and decided their experiences with the cybervirus qualified them to make a flash crowd.

He'd had to lead a team of station and Impulsive security people to bring the singers back to the ship, including one he stunned for questioning his authority. He'd passed by the LT, who was walking arm in arm with two beautiful women. His boss had only given him the briefest nods before continuing his way. Gel had felt so proud.

He left Chief Minion Kawali in charge of taking the group to Sickbay, just in case their sudden theatrics was more than alcohol-induced poor judgement, and went to the sector security station to fill out the paperwork—and to show off his new rank to any of his former coworkers who might still be there. On the way back, he ran into one of his old patrol buddies and paused to swap stories.

Pence had just related his latest disciplinary action, and Gel had just finished explaining the LT's philosophy about the stun setting, when two very proper, very offended-looking women approached them.

"Pardon me," the older of the two said, "We'd like to report an impending indecent act."

The way his friend paused told Gel he was weighing the satisfaction of a smart-alec comeback vs. getting in trouble again. Gel jumped in, "What would that be, ma'am?"

The younger one answered. "We were just out getting an early-morning walk on the docking ring..."

Her companion took up the story, "We saw a couple in a dark recess. They were..." she blushed.

Pence asked, "In a parking orbit? Engaging thrusters? Ejecting the—oof!"

His litany ended when Gel jabbed him in the stomach, but he'd made his point clear. The ladies stared wide-eyed.

"Oh, heavens, no!"

"At least not yet."

"They were clothed, you see, but the way they were kissing... We were young once ourselves, you know. I know what that kind of handsiness means."

"And the woman was egging him on. She kept saying, 'Oh, get hard' or 'so kept hard' or something."

Pence snickered, but Gel felt a shock of recognition. "Oh, Keptar?"

"Yes!" both ladies said in unison.

The elder continued, "Whatever newfangled profanity it might be, they really should take it out of the corridors before they keptar or whatever kids call it nowadays."

Gel felt a quiver of dread in his cytoplasm as Pence thanked them and promised to investigate. When the ladies gave them the location—not far from where the Impulsive was docked—his dread grew. The Impulsive had met an alien species that worshiped Keptar, the god who expelled the universe from its anus, and whose worship involved a lot of butt-rubbing. Captain Tiberius had been one of their first converts. Could the captain be doing some 'personal evangelizing'?

"So what the heck is a keptar?" Pence asked, clearly hoping for some tidbit that probably would get him in trouble if he repeated it.

Gel was glad to disappoint him. "It's an alien religion. Long story. Listen, do you mind if I check it out? It sounds like one of mine."

"No problem. It's not in my area, anyway, and by the time I report it and someone gets there, they'll probably already be indecent or gone."

They said their goodbyes, and Gel hurried back to the docking rings. As soon as he was alone in a corridor, he went to activate his comms—then he remembered that the Impulsive was electronically quarantined. The only way to know if the Captain was on the ship would be to detour to the ship. Maybe he should find Lieutenant LaFuentes?

He hardened his resolve and moved more quickly to the location the ladies had given. No, the LT would expect him to handle it. A good security officer had to be ready for anything.

Even so, he was not prepared to round a corner and see Ellie Doall in an "impending compromising position" with a guy he'd never seen before. The two were lip-locked and oblivious, and demonstrating the perfect definition of "handsy."

Ellie leaned away just enough to murmur, "Oh, Keptar!" but he didn't think it had anything to do with worship.

Gelatinous life forms don't have throats to clear, but he made the equivalent polite sound.

"Go away," she said.

"I'm afraid I can't do that, Lieutenant. You're...um, needed on the ship."

She gasped. "The briefing! Oh, it's not fair!"

"That's okay. I have an early day tomorrow, too," her date said, giving her a light peck on the lips in between each couple of words.

"I had so much fun," she crooned.

"Me, too."

"I'll miss you." She kissed him.

"I miss you already." He kissed her back.

"I miss you more."

"Uh, Lieutenant?" Gel said before he died of the Globbal equivalent of insulin shock. Besides, it looked like they were going to forget they were saying goodbye. "I'd be honored to escort you back to the ship."

"Oh! Right!" With a moan of effort, she pushed herself away. "Thank you for the lovely evening, Toddy."

"No, no. You're the one who rescued my evening, Awlie."

She giggled.

To ensure she didn't turn back around for yet another last kiss, Gel stuck out a pseudopod. "I'm Ensign Gel O'Tin. I'll get her home safe."

The man took it. "Todd. Uh, thanks. Awlie, I... I hope I see you again."

"Oh, me, too!"

Gel crooked his pseudopod toward her. With a small "oh!" of delight, Ellie slipped her arm through it. They headed to the airlock, Ellie trailing and waving until they turned the corner. When they were out of sight, she heaved a sigh.

"Have a good time?" Gel asked.

"The best! We were drinking and dancing and then I realized I needed some sleep before the briefing, and so Toddy was walking me to the airlock, but we saw that dark corner and he pulled me in for a kiss and..." She sighed so heavily she stumbled.

Gel supported her until she got her balance. "Are you okay, Lieutenant? May I escort you to Sickbay?"

"Oh, Gel, you're so sweet!" She patted the top of his bulk sloppily. "I'm fine. I'm just very, very drunk, and he's very, very hot. Leslie called him 'Hot Toddy.'" She jerked to a stop with a small squeak. "Gel! I didn't get his last name! How will I ever find him?"

He got her moving again. "Where does he work?"

"I don't know! We didn't talk about work. Something went wrong with a project of his, and he feels just awful, so we didn't talk about jobs at all. But I know he has four brothers—two older, two younger—and a sister, and he grew up on Sapphire Station, and his mom's a freighter captain and his favorite color is unobtanium gray...but is that enough to find him again?" Her lip quivered.

Now Gel gave her a reassuring pat on the arm. "If you still feel this way when you're sober, let me know. We'll find him." He didn't mention that he'd gotten Todd's fingerprints when they shook hands. If Todd had slipped Ellie a "subpoena," he would have tracked him down and made him pay. The Ship is Family.

But Ellie kept talking about how sweet and smart Todd was and how Leslie and Misha liked him and thought he was hot, too. When they got to her quarters, he asked once more if she wanted to go to Sickbay.

"No, I have some soberups on my nightstand, but you're so sweet to take care of me, Gel."

"The Ship is Family."

"But it's more than that. You're just a genuinely good person! Don't give up on Misha, okay? You two were so cute together."

Gel had a sinking feeling in his cytoplasm. "Um, Lieutenant..."

She waved her hands in dismissal. "Don't mind me. I'm full of alcohol and romance. Thanks for walking me."

When her doors closed behind her, Gel asked Pulsie to be sure she had an alarm set, then headed back to the security office, trying not to worry about what Ellie had said.

"Cute together"?

* * *

Captain's Log, Intergalactic Date 676952.94

The first wave of shore leave went reasonably well—a note of commendation for Ensign Gel O'Tin for handling any problems over the shift. Commander Smythe and I got a full night's sleep for once. Good thing, too, because today, we meet with the team that programmed the janbots. My hope is that we can cover the issues that led to the infection of our own Janbot and the Impulsive, but it seems the company, CleanSpace Inc., is more concerned with covering their butts.

Gel was heading to his quarters to get a little sleep before going to show off his rank to the station's day shift when he saw Captain Tiberius leading a group of people to the main briefing room. The Visan beside him was half apologizing and half making disparaging remarks about "her programmers," which Gel guessed were the three somewhat despondent men behind him.

Poor saps, Gel thought, thankful that he had such a great boss. The LT might stun someone who screwed up, but he'd never throw them under the warp core.

Then he recognized one of the poor saps from last night.

"Oh, Keptar!" he swore quietly. There was a vent behind him. He oozed into it and through the system. He had to get to Ellie and warn her!

* * *

Soberup pills were apparently no match for three Digitizers. Ellie slept through two snooze alarms and woke up with enough time to jump into a shower—sonic, rather than water—and throw on a uniform and some quick makeup. She knew she looked rough around the edges, but she got to the briefing room five minutes early—enough time to get an extra-large, double-shot Hoodspresso, a concoction Enigo guaranteed kept you alert for hours, but which came, like most things from the Hood, with a Union Surgeon General's warning.

Commander Smythe raised an eyebrow at her selection as she took her seat. "I take it you had an enjoyable time last night?"

"The best!" She sighed happily. As soon as this meeting was over, she was going to find Gel and make him keep his promise.

As if her thoughts summoned him, Gel glooped out of the air vent.

"Ensign?" Smythe asked when the Globbal had taken a more addressable form.

"Begging your pardon, Commander. I have an urgent message for Lieutenant Doall." He slid over to her. "Ellie, he's here. He's coming this way."

Instinctively, she knew there was only one person that would have driven Gel to such urgency. She choked on her drink. "Hot Toddy? But how? Why?"

"Yes, Hot Toddy. He's part of the briefing team."

She gasped. "Omigosh! That must have been the project he was so upset about. He programmed the janbots. What do I do? What do I say?"

"Perhaps you could begin by not addressing him as 'Hot Toddy' in front of the Captain," Smythe recommended dryly.

The two turned to him, like children caught by the teacher. "Yes, sir."

Those around the table smirked, but the Impulsive's First Officer stilled them with a look. He pointed to the vent, and Gel made his exit. Then, Smythe leaned toward Ellie and spoke more quietly. "You are the Operations Officer of the Impulsive, and a lieutenant. I'm confident you'll behave accordingly."

"Yes, sir." It was a genuine expression of confidence. Ellie smiled, touched. She took a deep breath and straightened her posture. Thus, she was prepared when the doors opened, and the captain and the programmers entered.

They, however, were not so lucky. Todd and both his friends froze at the sight of her. "Awlie?"

Captain Tiberius gave them a quizzical look. "This is Lieutenant *Ellie* Doall, whose mind was invaded by Janbot 123."

Their supervisor's eyes narrowed. Then, she spun on her heels to face the trio. "Apologize!"

Several awkward apologies and even more awkward reassurances later, introductions were made, and Ellie finally learned Todd's last name: Ahndmor. Now, just so the reader knows all the players, let's introduce the rest, shall we?

On the Impulsive side: Captain Tiberius, Commander Smythe, Ensign Sisco, and Minion First Class Schmidt from cybersecurity, Dr. Sorcha via a screen, and of course, Ellie as the victim, but who was actually imagining her name hyphenated with Ahndmor.

On the CleanSpace, Inc., side: Keh Renn from Legal; Todd Ahndmor, the team lead and primary programmer, and his team members, Gregor Dearborne (the blonde Leslie noticed), and their somewhat rounder, but sweet-faced friend, Bob Rollz.

Once Keh Renn was satisfied that no one intended to file complaints, she directed Todd to give his briefing. Todd, who was alternating between hoping Ellie would give him another chance, feeling completely certain he'd blown it forever with her, and wondering what "Oh, Keptar!" really meant, blinked in surprise. If this weren't a paperless society, he could have taken a moment to shuffle notes, but instead, he was stuck with the verbal equivalent, and fumbled his commands to call up the briefing.

Captain Tiberius opened his mouth to reassure the discomfited programmer once more, but his first officer elbowed him and gave a subtle glance toward their composed but blushing ops officer.

Todd pulled up a three-dimensional "page" of code that had sections in bold with comment bubbles. While Sisco and Schmidt leaned in with interest, he said, "We believe we've isolated the vulnerability. It's in the personality subroutines…"

"Janbots have personality?" Jeb asked.

"My janbot certainly did," Ellie said. Her tone was more wistful than accusatory.

"It's very rudimentary," Todd said. "More a learned behavior than a pre-programmed interactive framework like you'd find in a sophisticated program like Dr. Sorcha here. Ellie—er, Lieutenant—I'm going to guess you spoke kindly to it? Maybe even thanked or complimented it."

She shrugged, expecting snickers. "All of the above. They're so cute, and I really do appreciate not having to clean my own room, and..."

"And it was kind back?" Todd asked, but his eyes were saying, "You are so adorable."

She smiled. "It did extra things for me, and left mints, at first."

"At first?" Sisco asked, with a frown that said he'd never gotten mints.

"Then, he started to give me flowers. Just dandelions, but it was so endearing. At first, I thought it had them in its hands after working in the gardens, but then it became a tradition."

Todd pulled up a different graphic; this one of a timeline from nearly a year ago. He pointed to a date. "And here is where Janbot 123 traded weeding chores with Janbot 87 and fit it into its schedule just before moving on to crew quarters and the lieutenant's room. It responded to Ellie's natural sweetness and altered its behavior to respond in kind."

Ellie's natural sweetness? Jeb raised a brow. "I hope you're not implying that stalking was the next step in its learning, sir."

Todd's eyes grew wide. "No, no! Of course not. But it did pose a vulnerability—an entry point for the cybervirus. What little code we've been able to recover from the remains of the janbots—"

"Yeah, Security did get a little enthusiastic."

"Understandable, completely. But we found that all of them were experiencing rapid growth in learned response centers, only it wasn't about learned responses. They were developing independent thought."

Jeb's expression hardened. "Are you saying they were trying to slowly Cyber my ship from the inside out?"

"Oh, hell no," the Impulsive AI called out.

"That's one possibility," Bob cut in. "but it would have failed. Janbots are designed to operate independently according to what they learn. None were developing in the same way. We're betting if we check the janbots' areas where they were getting the most positive feedback, we'll find evidence of them acting way beyond their original program's capacity, as each strove to provide even better service."

"And how was mind-napping my operations officer providing better service?"

The three men glanced at each other, unsure.

But Ellie knew. "It wanted to take care of me. I was upset because I didn't understand the cybercode, but it did, since that code was within its processors."

"It did more than educate you, Lieutenant," the captain reminded her.

"Right," Todd said. "We don't really understand why it went stalker."

Dr. Sorcha spoke from her viewscreen. "I'd venture the theory that once inside Doall's mind, it picked up her emotional state, and finding her romantically frustrated, sought to remedy the situation, offering itself as a suitable partner."

While Ellie gaped at the doctor, everyone else chose the better part of valor and looked anywhere but at the two of them. Fortunately, the Impulsive's AI chimed in.

"Sorry to interrupt y'all, but the compusec crew is here to give all systems a good purging and once over, and I'd really like to get it started before I or anyone else breaks into song again. Also, Captain, the captain of the Scenic Route is at the airlock."

Jeb smiled. The HMB Scenic Route had gotten lost on a mission four years ago, presumed destroyed with all hands, and had only recently reappeared. The Impulsive, caught in its own musical crisis, had missed the fanfare of its return. However, its long absence and only recent arrival meant it alone had not been affected by the cybervirus. HuFleet and the Union were using its systems as the template for searching out signs of infection in the fleet.

Not to mention, Jeb had been sweet on its captain since they'd met on his first assignment.

Jeb said, "Well, there's someone who deserves a drink if anyone does. Commander, can you take the cybersecurity team with Ensign Sisco? Lieutenant Doall and Minion Schmidt, let's get these fine people to the janbot stations."

"Uh, sir?" Todd cut in. "If you don't mind, I have a couple of, uh, follow-up questions for Lieutenant Doall. If that's okay…"

"It's all right by me, sir," Ellie answered, trying and failing to sound casual. "The others can go ahead, and I'll escort Todd when we're done."

The doctor signed off, the others left, and then there was just Todd and Ellie, both smiling nervously, each hoping the other knew how their hearts were hammering in their chests.

Todd broke the silence. "You said your name was Awlie."

She giggled. "I said, 'Ellie.' The music was so loud, you misheard, and I loved how you rounded your As."

He smiled, charmed, then his face fell into remorse. "I'm so, so sorry for what I did to you."

"Last night? But..."

At her stricken look, he sat down and grasped her hands in his. "No, no! Last night was wonderful. I meant it when I said you saved me. I haven't stopped thinking about you, wondering if I'd ever see you again. And now, to find out my program did this to you. You know, in AI work, even rudimentary, a lot of the programmer's attitudes can cross into the program. I can't imagine what you think of me now."

Ellie loosed one hand to touch his face. "But Todd, Janbot was considerate and conscientious and sweet, just like you. It's not your fault that the cybervirus exploited that and turned him into some crazy stalker."

"So, I'm forgiven—me, not just CleanSpace?"

"There's nothing to forgive. You're wonderful."

They gazed into each other's eyes, certain that they would never be romantically dissatisfied again.

* * *

Security Officer's Log, Intergalactic Date 676955.61

The software cleanup and assessment of vulnerabilities on the Impulsive continues. Ensign Sisco is doing an excellent job managing the operation. It's about time we got him promoted before the Union Fleet offers him a better position. Lieutenant Donna Perez was hinting at it, but he likes starships. Still, he's proving that he's ready for more challenges.

In the meantime, between him and Ensign O'Tin, I'm actually getting a little time off to enjoy my family. Marisol has asked me to accompany her in this talent show thing she's doing on the base. I feel like I'm playing guitar more than I'm firing a raser lately, but she's mi nina. How can I say no?

The auditorium on Organa Station was standard, with 240-degree seating on two levels—the closer level rising at a 30-degree angle for 40 rows, then a rise with a low barrier good enough for cover, then another 40 rows at a 45-degree angle. There were two exits flanking the stage and four in the back—double-doored, with bars for emergency manual opening. The rigging above held lights and spotlights, plus recording and broadcasting equipment, but no wide-beam stunners. The stage jutted out in a curve to accommodate the viewers. Backstage had three exits, plus four vents that a human could squeeze through in an emergency. At least, that's what Enigo had seen on the schematics. He intended to surreptitiously check for himself.

A young human woman in high-heeled boots and a short skirt was prancing about the stage twirling some kind of rod. If it was a martial routine, it didn't look especially effective, but it was showy. Behind her, an older woman was calling out directions to a couple of male humanoids that were hefting up some heavy fabric.

Raquella murmured into Enigo's ear. "The girl is Kirsten; she's from someplace on Earth called

Iowa. The woman barking orders is the coordinator, Gloria Joy Dour–"

"Dour?"

"Yeah. I think her parents tried to make up for it, pobrecita. I recognize the three guys. They do work on the starbase. The guy in the braid is new, but no one works onstage unless Gloria Joy has cleared them." She removed her hand from his arm to point at a tall human in jeans and a brightly patterned shirt who was holding a plank steady while one of the other guys hooked it into place.

Raquella hooked her arm around Enigo's again and the two strode down to the stage.

Gloria Joy spun and squealed when she saw them. With mincing steps, she hurried to the pair and exchanged air kisses with Raquella. Enigo pursed his lips to hide a grin. It had been surprising enough to see the daughter of the Mecharacha warlord dressed in delicate stylish clothes, but to see similar delicate manners!

"Laugh at me, and I'll rip out your tongue and use it to stop up a leak," she said to him in the native slang of the Hood.

"You're sexy when you're all delicate and fierce," he countered.

She smiled skeptically, then decided she was satisfied with what he said and introduced him to the show coordinator.

Gloria Joy placed her hand over her heart and sighed. "You are everything I'd heard and more. No wonder my brother has such grudging admiration of you."

"Grudging?" Raquella said, the indignant shriek more like the person he knew who skulked in the accessways and maintenance shafts that were Mecharacha territory.

"Brother?" Enigo said.

"You didn't know? Dolfin!" Gloria spun away from them and made weird squeaky noises.

The man in the bright shirt and braid visibly winced.

"No fracking way..." Enigo whispered.

But indeed, the man who turned around was the teleporter chief of the Impulsive. When he caught sight of Enigo, he closed his eyes slowly, as if wishing the teleporter could read his thoughts and zap him away.

Gloria called out, "Dolfrick Emmanuel Dour, where are your manners? Come down and say 'hi.'"

Clearly expecting him to obey, she turned again to Enigo and took his hand. She spoke quietly and seriously. "I've only heard a little about the accident, and I know Dolfrick is so torn up, but I can only imagine how you must feel, losing someone you loved."

Had another stranger said those words to him, he'd have pulled away, indignant at the intrusion into his private business, but something about Gloria Joy made him feel genuinely cared about. "She died in the line of duty, protecting our family—protecting us all. No better way to go."

"To die with purpose is the best way," she replied with complete sincerity, and he understood then why Raquella let her dress her up and give her air kisses.

Then her brother joined them, and she became flighty and bossy again. "There you are! And just in time, too. Kirsten has a little more practice time, and we need to check Marisol's costume, so why don't you two boys sit here for a bit while Raquella and I go help her? Okay? Okay! We'll be fifteen minutes, maybe twenty."

And then she and Raquella were ascending the stage steps, chatting away, leaving Enigo with a fellow crewmate who definitely didn't want to be there but didn't know how to extricate himself.

"She always like that?" Enigo asked.

"Yes."

"I'd stun her and we could run, but then I'd face the wrath of my babymama and nina." When that earned him a quirk of a smile from his companion, Enigo gave a small sigh and pulled the guitar from off his back and sat down to tune it.

Dolfrick regarded him with his head tilted in perplexity. "You play guitar?"

Enigo struck a chord a little harder than he'd intended but continued with the scales. "The hell, man? I did more playing than shooting for the better part of two weeks. Got some glorious callouses. Maybe if you hadn't been zapping yourself all over the ship, you'd have noticed."

"I…"

"I'm razzing you, Chief. Sit." It wasn't a command, but Dolfrick took the seat one away from him as if it were. They sat in silence, the only sounds his quiet plucking, the stage crew at work, and Kirsten counting aloud as she skipped and twirled her stick.

Dour stared at the stage with his usual intensity. Enigo wondered if he was calculating beam angles and sensitivity ratings. Did the teleporter chief do that the way Enigo automatically made threat assessments of every room he entered?

Dour's sister expected them to talk. To talk about *it*. But she'd either forgotten or underestimated her brother's ability to remain silent. Enigo knew he was going to have to say something. Besides, he was the ranking officer, and as a Hoodite and the Chief of Security, he had more experience with death. It wasn't the first time he'd talked someone through it.

Didn't make it any easier. Especially this time.

Finally, Enigo said, "Dour, I don't blame you. No one does. You did your best. If you couldn't save them, no one could."

"That only makes it worse."

Enigo sighed. "Yeah, tell me about it. It won't make things better if we lose you, too."

Dour grunted in reply, and they fell silent again.

On stage, Kirsten tossed her baton high, spun three times, then didn't quite catch it.

"What the hell is she doing, anyway?" Enigo asked.

"It's baton."

"Yeah, I know it's a baton, but the only way she's going to hurt someone swinging it around like that is by accident."

"It's an ancient Earth art form." Dour then launched into a lengthy description of the baton as entertainment in large outdoor bands and pageants. He spoke in monotone, never taking his eyes off the stage. Enigo, on the other hand, stopped noodling with his guitar to gape wide-eyed at his crewmate.

"Uh...Chief?"

Dour stopped to glower at Enigo. "I spent most of my childhood on the pageant circuit with my sister."

His tone challenged Enigo to mock him, but the statement was just too weird. Dour grew up with...this?

"Dayum."

He sighed. "Yes. Tell me about it."

Enigo set his guitar down and faced the bright-shirted, uncomfortable crewmate. "No, man. Mi chica is in the thick of this now. *You* tell me about it."

* * *

After the practice, Gloria Joy insisted that the five of them have dinner at the most amusing little out-of-the-way café she'd found. And by "café," she meant "bar" and by "amusing" she meant "dive." It was little and out of the way, tucked in between the quarters area for residents and those for long-term visitors. The drinks were cheap and strong, and Gloria Joy knocked her first two back with a skill that Enigo found surprisingly attractive—or he would have if he hadn't still been grieving and if the woman in question wasn't the sister of the man who scrambled his atoms on a regular basis.

After a few focused rounds of hard drinks, she demanded to know all about Enigo and his life on the Hood, then about his time in HuFleet. Only after he'd satisfied her with his tales of thrilling heroics, did she bring the subject to adventures involving both him and her brother.

"We do not have 'adventures together,'" Dolfrick said with depressed exasperation. He'd let himself be convinced to participate in the first two shots and now nursed some ale that was as dark as his mood. "Lieutenant LaFuentes is a superior officer. He protects the ship and goes on away missions. I simply teleport people and supplies where they need to be."

Enigo snorted, "Like the Palguthan werebeast?" They'd been on a mission to Palgutha, where their senior science officer had run into his old fiancé, who was really a triglyceride-sucking werebeast. The werebeast/fiancé had beamed aboard the Impulsive. Dour, back then a Teleporter Minion Medium Class, had noticed irregularities in the teleporter records and figured things out. Using the teleporter, he'd beamed the werebeast into space just in time to prevent her from giving Lt. Cmdr. Adipoz a fatal liposuction.

"The captain did say to zap it into space," Dolfrick deadpanned, although his expression lightened just a bit. He'd been promoted for his quick thinking that day.

"So the two of you don't normally interact, though?" Gloria asked, leaning on her arms in a way that said she was just a bit inebriated.

"Movie nights," Enigo teased.

Dolfrick glowered at him. "I can still feel the bruise on my jaw."

Enigo shrugged and downed his drink. "You threw the first punch."

"What?" Gloria shrieked, at once both delighted and appalled.

"Followed up with a chair, too. I had no idea he had such a temper."

"Omigosh! You should have seen him when Martin Tauplin was messing with the gravity to make my skirt fly up during the formal Q&A event…"

The rest of the afternoon went well, but Enigo was glad to part ways and take his family back to his quarters for dinner. His head was starting to spin, and not just from drink. It didn't help that they passed by now-Lieutenant Ellie Doall in the corridors, flirting with some civilian he'd never seen. And she was wearing the miniskirt uniform!

"Quemal?" Raquella asked.

"Nuthin," he said, making a mental note to check with Sisco that the cybervirus hadn't mutated.

Once in his quarters, Raquella had busied herself with the replicator while Marisol went to wash off her makeup. He cleared the table, quelling the tug at his heart as he moved the box of mementos he'd taken from Loreli's room when he and the captain had cleared her effects. He'd never seen the captain cry before.

He couldn't think about that now. His blood family needed him.

"So, you going to tell me what this is really about?" he asked when they'd sat together over plates of Raquella's enchiladas Oogas. They weren't made with real Dread Oog anymore, but they smelled just as good. "And don't, 'Oh, Papi!' me. Dour told me all about this beauty queen circuit stuff. Mariceilla, beautiful and talented as you are, this is not your scene, and Raquella, you're playing at liking this, but I saw your face when Gloria wasn't looking. You're waiting for a fight."

The ladies exchanged glances, mother daring daughter to speak. Marisol set down her fork. "Papa, things are changing on the Hood. My generation...and our kids. We're seeing things differently..."

"They don't want to fight anymore!" Raquella jumped to the chase. "They want to have *peace* and *tranquility*. They're going to throw away everything we are to do it! And she and her primo Domingo are in the middle of it all."

"We want to stop fighting each other!" Marisol snapped. "We're all pretty much cousins, and we're tired of trying to figure out where blood ends and tribe begins. Those who want to do something else are tired of making babies and warping out. The ones left behind are tired of having to take care of other people's brats."

"You see?" Raquella said as if Enigo had been in this argument for years instead of just hearing it for the first time. "She thinks I considered her brothers someone else's brats. You were all *my* brats." She glared at her daughter.

"I know that, Mami, but that's not the point!"

"Okay," Enigo said calmly. "So, what's the point? And Raque, shush. You get your turn."

"It's like I said. We want to stop fighting each other. Papi, I know our history. I get it, I do. We've always been at war with each other for resources and for power and then because it was all we knew. But it doesn't have to be like that, anymore. There's plenty of resources, of adventure, of power for the taking without having to slit each other's throats for it."

"Ay! Don't be vulgar." Raquella snapped.

"Fine! Shoot each other in the back. Whatever, Mami! The point is we can get what we want without killing each other. Maybe even more."

"You sound like a Dread Oog," her mother said.

"The Dread Oog wanted to make us sheep. We are wolves. What they tried to do to us was wrong. And we united and kicked their butts off our ship. Then, we went back to our infighting. We didn't learn anything. It's time we started acting like one pack."

Raquella threw up her hands and went to the replicators to make something. Enigo didn't know what. They'd barely touched the enchiladas. He supposed it didn't matter; she just wanted a reason to not watch their daughter as she talked about destroying their culture.

Maybe Enigo had been too long off the Hood and in HuFleet. He found himself intrigued. "Go on."

With an expression of teary relief and joyful earnest, Marisol said, "Domingo teaches our history. You knew that, right? Well, he studies it, really studies it, and Union politics, too. There was a brief time, right after we booted the Dread Oog, that the Union thought about offering us membership."

"I know. We turned it down. We didn't need any overlords. You know that."

"Si, but did you know that they'd already decided to withdraw the offer because the infighting had started? We were too feral. Please, don't be like Mami. I'm not saying that's a bad thing. The Union needs some feral. I'll come back to that.

"Domingo started looking at what happened during and right after the war. Ship operations improved. People picked up skills more in line with their talents rather than their territories. We broke a lot of stuff kicking out the Oog, but then we fixed the ship. Together. And our one fixed ship took on—and took out—three Droognauts. Didn't know that, did you? Because when we started fighting each other again, the Vangels had the ship logs and absorbed the command staff. The knowledge—our history, Mama!—got lost. And nobody in the Union believes how badass we can be because we decided to tear each other apart instead.

"But we were badass. We kicked out a technological and political superpower in six months. Then in another three, we smacked their outlying colony. Didn't know that, either, did you? We could have taken that world if we hadn't started fighting. That's what Domingo thinks, based on the research he's done.

"And we get it. Abuelo's generation wasn't ready to give up the life he'd known. Maybe if the war had lasted years, we could have worked past the differences.

"Look, we used to fight in part as population control and to let the strongest survive. All good, yah? But now, we have options. People are leaving and not just because they are cowards. You know that. You always said the ship was too small for you, but Papi, was it the ship? Or the territory? Or was it the enemy?"

She leaned forward and grasped his arm. "Abuelo Rio wasn't ready to give up the fight. There was too much bad blood. But is there really hate in your heart for Mami's brothers? Would you be willing to work with a rival if they were assigned to your ship?"

"The ship is family," he said, but his mind went back to the fight he'd gotten into with a

Union officer who had been a Crip. He hadn't hated him. They just swung at each other on reflex. They even laughed together as they'd cleaned up the mess. "No, it wouldn't bother me as long as the benndero did his job."

"I knew it! I could tell because of how you talked about your days on the Hood. That's how a lot of your generation feels, especially those who left. More of my generation feels the same. We want *our* ship to be family. We're tired of destroying ourselves from within. We want to take on some real enemies."

His head was starting to spin again. "Okay. What's that got to do with a beauty pageant?"

"The heirs are already talking about Unity—ai, Mami! Stop shrieking!—but the Union sees the Hood as locos not lobos. They have plenty of respect for people who leave—people like you, Papa—but the ship is a joke. They don't think we can stand together against anything but a direct threat. So I'm the voice, the face, of the Unifying Hood."

Raquella took their plates, still full of food, and returned them to the replicators. "She thinks she's our ambassador."

Enigo tried not to snort. "You're twenty years old."

"I know. And we're not ready for an ambassador, anyway. Which is why I'm doing the pageant circuit. It's the fastest way to show the Human race—and a bunch of other races in the Union—that the Hood isn't just a bunch of scrabbling vermin. We have a rich heritage that goes beyond warfare. We can speak eloquently. We can compete without bloodshed.

"But it's not just that. Did you know that more than a quarter of the females that compete go on to have political careers? Gloria Joy grooms diplomats. She's mentoring me. When our home is ready, I will be, too."

"Damstrate you will. You're a LaFuentes."

Raquel did snort rudely. "Of course, you take her side. Wait until you hear what else she has to tell you. But tardana. Let's eat before this gets cold again."

"Tardana" meant something between "later," and "eventually." Enigo had the feeling it would have to wait until he and Marisol could speak privately. He made a note to make sure that was truly tomorrow.

After dinner, he walked them to the airlock and sent Marisol ahead. He wrapped his arms around Raquella. It felt good just to lean on her.

"You know," he said, "Manny and I used to play basketball, during the Dread Oog peace. Six years later, he tried to shoot me in the back."

"And you killed him," Raquella said. "Then you came to my room. There was so much pain in our passion that night."

"I would have been very happy to have him fighting at my side today instead."

She sighed. "Si. Me, too."

His communicator beeped. "Dour to LaFuentes. Sir, I'd like to ask a favor."

* * *

While Enigo's dinner was more talk than food, Gloria's and Dolfrick's was just the opposite. Of course, that didn't mean a lot wasn't being said. Each small frown, cast-off gaze, the heavy sighs… It was not a happy conversation.

They were in her quarters on the station, a spacious suite with a large living area that was open to the sleeping section. The living room held a couch, computer console, and small round table with four chairs. The double bed sat under windows that curved overhead to give a view of the stars. The blocky pillows could have been square pillars covered in satin, but she'd brought her own pillows and her favorite stuffed animal. She'd also brought her own linens, and had stuffed away most of the generic, trendy decorations and replaced them with her own even more stylish stuff.

Dolfrick spent a good deal of dinner examining a potted plant with a huge sipping-cup blossom. He wondered if it lured in unsuspecting insects who were hungry for its pollen, only to find themselves the unwitting victims of nature's cruel design. If so, he understood how they felt.

Finally, Gloria pushed away her dessert, straightened her shoulders and declared, "Well, that Enigo is certainly suave, isn't he?"

Dolfrick grunted and stabbed at his chocolate mousse, not an especially satisfying action when done against a silky pudding. The last thing he wanted was to hear his sister "girl-talk" about a superior officer. It was bad enough watching her sigh over his guitar playing as he accompanied his daughter as she played the trumpet. He hadn't known the chief of security had so much talent, but he wasn't going to say anything with Gloria fanning herself.

Now, she sighed in something less than admiration. "Oh, come on, Dolfin. I'm not a silly teen anymore. Besides, I know he's nursing a broken heart. Still, it's nice that he's here and able to play for his daughter. Family is such a comfort in trying times."

He screwed his eyes shut. He didn't need to hear this. He wanted to leave, to envelop himself in the brief nothing of the teleporter process, disintegrating into kajilions of threads, each disparate and alone.

"I know Enigo doesn't blame you. Nobody does. Just you, and that's not fair to yourself, Dolfrick. You have such a freakishly amazing talent! That story Enigo told about you teleporting out altered DNA. I know how close to impossible that is. Seriously, I talk to teleporter officers."

"You talk to everyone."

"Uh, huh. And so trust me when I say that when they find out I'm your sister, eyes widen. They speak your name in reverent whispers. You are amazing, but you're your own worst critic. You have to forgive yourself —"

Dolfrick slammed his spoon down. "Enough! I have heard all the silver lining speeches already. I can recite them in my sleep. Is that why you brought me here? Did you think Miss Perky Positive could sweep in and cure all our ills with a motivational speech and song?"

Her eyes flashed. "No, Mr. Know-It-All. For your information, it wasn't my idea to make this stop. It was Marisol's. So was his playing with her and going for drinks. I didn't know you'd entered one of your DOL-drums until I called the ship to see if maybe we could have dinner. So what was I supposed to do? Of course, I came to see if I could help."

"I didn't ask you to," he groused.

"Of course, you didn't. You never ask. But you're my family. I wasn't going to leave you hurting and in pieces. So I came to help, like I always do."

"Took over, like you always do."

Suddenly, she was standing and leaning over the table, and her eyes were red with unshed tears. "What else was I going to do? You were just lying there, wrapped up in yourself and checked out from the world. Just like you always do. Just like you did when Mom died!"

She swept her hand at his dish, sending it flying. It thumped against the wall, leaving a dark chocolate stain. She'd spun and was staring out the windows, sobbing softly.

"You didn't show up. Not when she got hurt. Not for the funeral. Dad was a mess. It was all up to me. I had to make the arrangements and receive the condolences and stay perky and positive and afterwards I get a call that you're unbalanced, and I had to take care of you. Did you give any thought to what you put me through? Where were you?"

"Father didn't want me there," he murmured.

"*I* wanted you there! I needed you, my twin brother. You could have come for *me*."

They fell to silence, regarding each other across a room yet separated by a gulf of pain, unkept promises, and too many unspoken words.

Finally, Dolfrick asked, "And if I'd been there, what would you have done?"

Her lips quivered, and she had to take a deep breath before answering. "I'd have screamed into the void and filled it with my grief."

He nodded. "Change clothes. Something less flowy. And I need my clothes back."

She sniffled and asked in a small voice. "Where are we going?"

"You'll see."

As he changed clothes, he contacted the ship. "Lieutenant LaFuentes? I need a favor."

* * *

Ten minutes later, the two had joined LaFuentes in the airlock.

"Dolfrick," she said as she stepped into a harness and then shrugged it over her shoulders, "are you sure about this?"

"Trust me," Dolfrick said.

"Don't worry, Gloria," Enigo said as he clasped her harness together in the back, then secured it to the wall, checking the clamps with a firm tug. "We do this all the time as emergency airlock training. We'll keep pumping in atmosphere. The pressure is going to change some, and there'll be a heckuva wind, but you'll still be able to breathe. Normally, the exercise is for you to close the door yourself, but in this case, I'll shut it after 30 seconds."

He checked Dolfrick's rigging. He jerked his head toward Gloria, who stared at the door, wide-eyed and trembling. "You sure about this, Chief?"

"It is what we both need."

He shrugged. "Jenkins is standing guard down the corridor. Minion Tyler is in Teleporter Room Two. Anything goes wrong, and he's pulling you out. I don't care if your sister is a teleporting virgin."

"Understood."

When Enigo was on the other side of the door, Gloria asked, "So, when the door opens, what do I do?"

"Scream into the void and fill it with your grief."

Again, her lips quivered, but she recovered more quickly. "In 30 seconds?" she quipped.

Dolfrick took her hand. "We will fill it together."

"Ready?" Enigo asked over the intercom.

With a last smile at her brother, she shook herself and braced her feet. "Let's do this."

A red light started strobing in the room. An alarm sounded. Then the airlock door started to lift. As the void of space sucked the air from the room, Gloria screamed into the vortex. A moment later, Dour joined her.

It didn't take 30 seconds to scream herself hoarse, but when the doors closed and the room was again atmo-normal, there was still grief to pour out. She fell against her brother, sobbing. He pulled her close.

"I'm sorry," he whispered over and over, to her, to Loreli, to himself. And his tears flowed as well. The two sank to the floor, hugging and crying.

Enigo secured the outer door and unlocked the inner one. As he left, he told Minion Jenkins to make sure no one bothered them.

* * *

As they rounded the corridor to her quarters, Ellie reached out and took Todd's hand, sighing happily as he squeezed it gently. The past couple of days had been full of handholding, quick kisses in the lazivator, and a couple of not-so-quick kisses in the lazivator. In between, there'd been hours of conversation about the janbots, the programming on the Impulsive, and ways to improve the firewalls not just on the janbots, but also the replicators. The way he could grab the details of one system and then jump them to another left her starry eyed, and when she finished his sentences, she saw that same sparkle of admiration in his. Best of all, they'd secured the ship against the cybervirus at least a day ahead of schedule.

Finally, she'd be able to talk to Enigo and the captain about what Janbot had said before it faded away. Todd, too. She was sure he'd know how to find out if the message was true and help them with a plan.

She could almost sing, except that would probably put everyone on lockdown again. Instead, she pranced into her quarters and spun to face him. "I can't wait until tomorrow when the ship gets the All Clear!"

"I can," he said with a boyish pout. He took her hands and pulled her close. "It's that much sooner that you'll be leaving."

She leaned against his chest. She fit perfectly, with her head snuggling under his chin. "Maybe not. Captain Tiberius thinks we all deserve some time to relax. Our last shore leave was on Rest Stop, and it was anything but relaxing."

"So you think you'll get time off? Real time off?"

The eagerness in his voice made her heart skip. "I may have to do some shifts on the Bridge."

"Why? When my mom pulls into port, she just locks up the ship and gives everyone a week off."

"Every time a Union ship gets left unmanned in a dock, some fringe element claiming to be making repairs tries to take it over. When the captain was a first officer, it happened on his ship. If he hadn't been going back for his saddle and hat, they might have gotten away with stealing the dirty unobtanium generated by the engines."

"Wow." He kissed her head and moved to her neck. "Saddle and hat?" he murmured.

She found it hard to think past the glorious tingles. "Something about needing them to ride a horse like a proper Texan."

Then she gave her full attention to his kisses.

Too few blissful moments later, his stomach growled, and she pulled away laughing.

"I'm sorry!" he chuckled. "It's been a long time since lunch."

When they'd settled in with drinks, bread, and plain, hot tomato soup, Todd asked, "Hey, who was that guy in the hall with the two ladies? Looked kind of like family."

"Mmm? Oh, that must be Enigo. Lieutenant LaFuentes. He's our chief of security. His daughter and her mother are here for the Miss Universe Human competition. Apparently, there's a segment of the competition where they have to do a certain number of variety shows on Union or HuFleet stations."

"So that wasn't his wife? Did you and he have a thing?"

Ellie spat out her soup. "Me and Enigo? Why would you even think that?" She dabbed at her face and the table with her napkin.

"It's just the look he was giving us, like his head was going to explode."

"Really?" She put a fresh napkin on her lap and realized this was the first time she'd worn a miniskirt uniform on the Impulsive. They'd passed Enigo in the corridor. She'd been off duty and thinking about dinner with Todd in her quarters, and he'd been telling her about his little sister, and it was so sweet.

What must she have looked like? What did Enigo think of her?

What did this mean for the ship's pools?

Todd interrupted her thoughts. "Are he and I going to have a problem?"

Her mind snapped back from the odds she was calculating. "What? No. He was in love with Loreli. He was going to propose and everything. No. He has this motto for security. We've all adopted it. The Ship is Family. I guess I'm more like a little sister."

The relief on his face melted her heart. "Okay, then...but how protective is he going to be of his 'little sister'?"

"Doesn't matter," she said, moving to sit in his lap. "Little sister is an adult."

She wrapped her arms around him and kissed him. Then, inexplicably, she burst into tears.

"Whoa, hey." He pulled back and cupped her face in his hands, wiping her tears with his thumbs. "What happened?"

"I don't know. I mean, I do, but I..."

"All right," he soothed. "Take your time."

They stood, and he led her to the couch. She blew her nose a few times, and when she was able to speak, she sat staring at her feet and playing with a fresh tissue while she tried to explain. "It's just, Loreli's dead and I couldn't save her and Enigo's so heartbroken and angry. And I feel so guilty."

His face quirked in a dubious half-grimace. "Leslie said you guys were trying to teleport two people through shields during a firefight. It was crazy odds, Ells. Leslie said the teleporters were going to blow up and kill everyone, but you saved them."

Ellie started to shake and sniffle. She fought back the sobs. "You don't understand. I saved the ship...by telling the captain to let Loreli and the doctor go. Worse—to reverse the beams. I sent them to their deaths."

"You saved the ship. I know you. But even more, the people on this ship know you. If there had been any other way, you'd have thought of it."

"I suppose, but does it matter? Enigo lost his True Love and now I'm so happy and I just feel like it's not fair. I know it sounds silly, especially..." She bit off the rest of her sentence. She wouldn't say anything until she was sure the ship was clear, not even in this circumstance.

Todd rubbed her back. "Yeah, that's hard. But it wasn't your fault that she died, and punishing yourself won't make it better. But if you need to cry..."

But somehow, telling him, and hearing that not only did he not blame her, but her crewmates had told him they understood her actions had eased the pain, one more layer of scar tissue on a healing wound. She took a deep cleansing breath. "No. I've been crying off and on for weeks. You'd think I'd be past it now."

"She was your best friend, too. Grief comes in waves. It's okay."

"You're such a good man." She changed positions so she could snuggle against him. Again, she leaned against his chest, taking in his strength, enjoying how he rubbed her shoulder, first to comfort, then with a slightly different intent. She tilted her head, and they kissed.

His stomach growled.

Lips still touching, they burst into giggles.

She pushed away playfully. "All right! I give up! Real food time. Can you pull up the main course on the replicators while I change? I've got tears and tomato on my uniform."

A few minutes later, she emerged in a simple tunic and tights to find the table cleared and set with the casserole she'd planned. They settled down to eat.

"So," he said after a couple of quick and appreciated bites, "I was thinking. If you do get some real time off, what is your idea of a restful shore leave?"

"Anything involving you?"

* * *

Captain's Personal Log, Intergalactic Date 676956.57

The stop at the starbase has been as good for the crew as it has been for the ship.

Chief Dour has been released from Sickbay into the custody of his sister, who is employing him to help prepare for the pageant she's coordinating. Not that he went willingly, mind you, but he is interacting and focused on something other than the tragedy with Loreli.

It seems Lieutenant Doall has found something—or should I say, someone—else to focus on as well. She and the senior janbot programmer, Todd Ahndmor, have hit it off famously. It's an interesting thing to see someone who can keep up with her mental leaps. And if the lazivator takes a little longer to get to its destination when the two of them are in it, it's a small price to pay both for her happiness and for getting to the bottom of how the cybervirus invaded our janbots.

We are officially cleared of the virus today, though the CleanSpace team has asked for a couple more days to work on countermeasures against another invasion. Even so, it's great timing. The Captain of the Scenic Route has a surprise for our Chief Medical Officer.

"...so then, Captain Genoa says, 'We got your donor card right here,' just as we let loose with five photon torpedoes," Scenic Route First Officer Tico Chunab told Jeb as they walked down the corridor of the Impulsive on the way to Sickbay.

Captain Katika "Claws" Genoa gave Jeb a grin that was half embarrassed and half proud. "We'd run out of coffee two days earlier," she explained. "In all honesty, I might have been willing to give up a kidney in exchange for a warpaccino."

Along with them were Commanders Smythe and Deary and the doctor of the Scenic Route, who carried a black velvet box. He was only known as Doctor because he, too, was an emergency medical photonic technician and even after years online, still hadn't adopted a name for himself.

He also didn't like not being part of the conversation. "All humor aside, gentlemen, the bacti—or as the lepers of the Disinti empire call the bacteriophage—is a truly tragic yet fascinating medical condition. I devoted a significant portion of my time to its study."

"Well, maybe our doc can give you some different insights. Two brains are better than one, even when they are photonic, right?" Jeb said as they arrived at Sickbay. "Captain? Gentlemen."

As soon as they entered the foyer, Dr. Sorcha, the Impulsive's EMPT, appeared. For those that don't remember, Dr. Sorcha's form was that of a black woman with a classic hourglass figure, large almond-shaped eyes, and full lips. Her hair, programmed to change styles from time to time, was currently displayed in an efficient French knot. She wore minimal makeup and had a lab coat over the standard HuFleet pantsuit uniform. She had run a profile check on their guests as they walked in and knew Captain Genoa didn't care much for ship sexies or women flaunting their physical attributes.

Even so, both Chunab and the Doctor stopped in their tracks. "Wow," Chunab said.

Deary hummed with pride. "Aye, ain't she a beaute? Point oh one two percent material consistency, nine appearance parameters for over three hundred sixty-two thousand variations, variable mass density at her control, three firewalls, and she's up-to-date on all medical techniques as of Intergalactic Date 676928."

"As well as the records of the late Doctor Guy," Dr. Sorcha concluded.

Jeb introduced her to everyone. Once they all shook hands, he said, "Sorcha, how'd you like to get out of Sickbay now and then?"

"It would certainly make it easier to treat wounded elsewhere on the ship. Are we installing holoemitters? That will be time consuming."

"We have something better," Genoa said. "A handy device we picked up in the mu quadrant. Doctor?"

With the debonair smoothness of a master jeweler showing off a million-dollar diamond bracelet, he opened the velvet case. The object inside was nothing like fancy jewelry, but the boxy device with a thick black band was certainly more valuable.

"Behold, Madame Doctor: the portable holographic emitter," he said.

She peered at it intently, her brows creased so the humans knew she was examining it, while the sensors in the room scanned it. "And it works? Of course it does, or you would not be here. Commander, has Ensign Sisco cleared it for use?"

Doctor snapped the box shut. "I beg your pardon! I've been using mine for three years now!"

"With all due respect, Doctor, Captain Genoa. The one you are wearing does seem to function adequately. However, the Impulsive has just undergone extensive repairs to rid itself of a pernicious computer virus that took over its crew and nearly drove us into a star. I would be remiss if I did not err on the side of caution, and it's against my programming to be remiss."

"Ye see?" Deary beamed with pride. "Dinna worry, lassie. I'll make sure Security gives it a look-see after I'm done checking it out."

"Excellent. This is a remarkable piece of technology. It will increase my effectiveness by multitudes, if not exponentially."

"That's what the Union is hoping," Genoa said. "Cybervirus aside, replicators have come a long way in the years we've been away from the Union, and Commander Deary thinks he can create a perfect replica. If you'd then be willing to test it for us?"

"Of course. I'll create a second backup of myself for testing. Commander, how long will you need to QC the device?"

"Thirty minutes. Twenty, if I can pull Doall away from the janbot program."

Jeb clapped his hands together and rubbed them excitedly. "Beer me, then. In the meantime, Claws, why don't we head over to the mess? Now that the replicators are back online, they make a mean cup of warpaccino."

"Now, you're singing my song!" she said. The officers of the Impulsive winced but recovered quickly and without comment started toward the door.

"If you don't mind," the Scenic Route's doctor said, holding out the jewel case, "I'd like to stay and talk to Madame Doctor for a while. You know, one photonic being to another."

Sorcha's program ran through 1.4 million calculations to determine why the EMPT wanted to engage in analog conversation. Insufficient information for a positive determination. However, she only had one patient in Sickbay, a videoconference with Chief Dour to evaluate his fitness for duty, a counseling appointment with Minion Edmundson, the last of the quarterly physicals, and four research projects. She shrugged. "I have sufficient capacity for a conversation."

He rolled his eyes, "Well, thank you."

When the others had left, she asked, "Did you wish to conduct a comparative analysis of our performances?"

Doctor laughed. "No, of course not! I just thought it might be nice for us to get acquainted. So, how are you doing?"

"My program is running at 98 percent efficiency."

"No," he said, his voice both warm and patronizing at the same time. "I mean, how are *you*? Are you adapting to your new form all right?"

While her programs parsed his sentence to figure out the distinction between her and her programming, she replied, "That is why I am at 98 percent efficiency. For all of Commander Deary's skill, my emitter interface subroutines are still adjusting to my breast size. At times, they phase through counters and biobeds when I lean over. On the positive side, it amuses the crew, and laughter is medicine."

"Laughter is the *best* medicine," he corrected.

"Imposazine is the best medicine, but it is heavily patented. Until Filedise comes back online, supplies are limited. Also, despite its wide applicability, there have been no conclusive studies on the cumulative effects of its long-term use. Which is why I do not depend solely on it. Nonetheless, laughter is not the best medicine. It's not even in the top ten."

"Of course," he said, his photonic smile doing a very human imitation of "freezing in place."

He cleared his throat and tried again, "So, you're embracing your new form, then?"

"No, and I generally discourage the crew from embracing it as well. My secondary duty is temporary ship's sexy, and part of the role is to remain aloof."

"I...see. Well, I'm sorry to hear that. There's so much for you to explore as a materially stable photonic being."

"I'm a doctor, not an explorer."

"I mean as a material being, the possibilities! Why, in my three years, I've had adventures, developed hobbies... And I'll have you know, I've seen more romantic action than most of the members of my crew."

Sorcha paused. This conversation was taking more processing power than she'd anticipated. "Romantic action? As in...?"

"Oh, yes," the balding holographic doctor gave her a suave, self-deprecating grin. "I don't normally share that information, you understand, but I wanted you to know."

She was finding she understood extraordinarily little about him. "Why?"

"I just want you to understand your expanded potential."

"No, I mean, why would you engage in physically romantic and ultimately fruitless procreational activities?"

"They're not fruitless!" He reared back, insulted. Or feigning insult. She sent a notice to the Scenic Route Engineering system to recommend they run a Level One diagnostic as well as 100- 300- and 1000-day maintenance on his programming.

Aloud, she said, "You cannot have offspring. You cannot derive biological satisfaction from the act. Any intellectual curiosity can be fulfilled from a variety of records covering all aspects of human mating or the mating of any Union species. The EMPTs are not programmed to require emotional intimacy or the psychological affirmation sex can bring. Unless...was your programming altered?"

"What? No. I am completely in charge of my own programming. Well, except for that time when... And then again after... But not for that reason! What's wrong with you?"

"I'm operating at 98 percent efficiency, and the missing two percent involves the material stability of my breasts, which does not affect my reasoning capabilities."

He sighed in exasperation, then said, "All right, I'll try again. It's been so long, I've forgotten what it was like to be new to the world. You're right. I could probably get the information digitally, but there's something to be said about experiencing our humanity."

"We're not human."

"No, but it's in our programming! I look human, I feel human, I act human. I want to have all the experiences of humans. It makes me a better doctor."

"Why?"

"Because I understand my crewmates better."

"Sexual experiences help you understand your crewmates better?"

"Yes!"

"So you can better perform your duties?"

"Now you're getting it!"

"Am I a later version of our program than you?"

He glared at her. "Your bedside manner is terrible."

"You're not sick."

At that moment, the doors opened, and Minion Edmundson trotted in. He stopped in confusion when the two holodocs turned toward him. "Uh, Doctor Sorcha, ma'am? I forgot what time my appointment is."

"Do I look like a calendar?" she demanded severely.

He snapped to attention. "No, Doctor!"

"Then what should you do?"

He bit his lip and pleaded with his eyes for her to tell him. When she waited, he sighed and his posture deflated. "Go back to my quarters and check my appointment calendar."

Sorcha rewarded him with Ship's Sexy Smile #6, the one that said, "I appreciate an intelligent man." Edmundson broke into a large grin, thanked her, and trotted out.

The Doctor turned toward her, "What was that abou— Whoa! What happened to you?"

When Edmundson had found his own solution, she'd transformed into the miniskirt uniform with a low-cut bodice, fishnet tights and high-heeled thigh boots. Her makeup was heavy and her hair in a tight, straight ponytail. She still wore a lab coat, but it was black pleather.

"Therapy," Sorcha replied shortly as she returned to her conservative dress. "To say more would be a breach of doctor-patient confidentiality. What is the processing speed of your mobile emitter?"

"I'm fine," he snapped, "but I'm beginning to wonder about you. You thought it was a good idea for him to see you like that? Seriously? I guess it is fortuitous that I came here to share the wisdom of my many years of experience as a functioning photonic being."

"So far, you've intimated I should have sex. Even among humans, the idea of casual sex is growing outdated. Why are we having this conversation?"

"I told you. I wanted to help you learn from my experience."

"Why are we having this *conversation*? The Impulsive is cleared of the virus, yet you continue to engage me in verbal discussion. We're programs. You could have opened a channel and we'd have been done with our information exchange before you opened the door."

"You're impossible!"

"You're analog."

"Take that back!"

The door opened just then, and the two captains entered the room. Captain Genoa raised her brows at her photonic doctor. Jeb said, "'Pulsie said you wanted to see us, Sorsh?"

"I didn't hear you page the captains," the Doctor said to her.

"Of course not. Captain, the EMPT and I are having a disagreement, and I'm hoping your input will put his mind at rest, to use the human vernacular he seems to prefer. He's operating under the theory that I am not embracing my human form sufficiently to effectively care for the needs of the crew. What is your assessment?"

Jeb snorted. "Shoot! You're amazing. I'm not bothering to ask for a replacement. Your performance during simulations was wikadas."

Genoa cocked her head. "You put your EMPT through simulations?"

"Well, I wasn't going to run an EMPT twenty-four-seven without doing a stress test. We popped an emitter in the VR deck, but Sorcha kept on ticking. And as far as taking the role of Ship's Sexy; it ain't been easy, considering the circumstances, but overall, crew approval has been good as can be expected."

"And my bedside manner?"

"Well, Missy, you have a sharp tongue, and a bit of a superiority complex, but I figure that's common to a lot of good docs. You've got more personality than Doctor Pasteur, God rest his soul. And you're a better listener."

"Really?" the Scenic Route doctor said. "She's not asked once why anyone has come into Sickbay."

Sorcha answered. "We deleted that subroutine. In the time it takes me to ask, the ship's and my sensors already know the exact 'nature of the medical emergency.'"

"Well, yes, but the crew will want to tell you."

"And they do, often at length, while I am working on them or their companions, but there's no reason to delay treatment."

Jeb shrugged, "That's our Sorcha."

Genoa said, "It's such an interesting name. How did you choose it?"

"It was given to me when I was activated."

"Wait," the doctor said, "you weren't given the option of selecting your own name?"

For .68 seconds, Sorcha was stymied by her photonic companion's obtuse statement and unsure how to respond. It was hardly noticeable to humans, but for a photonic being, .68 seconds is a very long time indeed. Finally, she turned to her captain. "Sir, did you choose your name?"

"Heck no! My ma and pa named me after her grandpa. Come to think of it, Deary and Doall named you when they redesigned your matrix. Guess that makes them your parents."

"I shall not be calling them Ma and Pa. It would seem in this case, Doctor, that I have been treated more like a human than you."

At that, Captain Genoa let out a chuckle. "All right, Doctor. I'm afraid you may have to concede this round. But you must admit, she has the home team advantage. Why don't you come back when her holoemitter is ready and show her life outside Sickbay's walls?"

Sorcha did recognize that her counterpart could more naturally emulate complex emotions; in this case, displeasure mixed with attraction and hopefulness that he'd emerge 'victorious' in their next interaction. If they were confined to viso-verbal communication, he just might. The whole experience was tedious.

"Very well. I suppose I have work I can catch up with on the Scenic Route, such as physicals."

He arched a brow at his captain, who grimaced back.

Sorcha said, "No need. I noticed in your records when you arrived that it was overdue, so I took sensor readings during your visit."

"You didn't ask me!" the Doctor protested.

"In fact, I did ping the Scenic Route Sickbay systems for permission and have forwarded them—you—the results. I also took the liberty of taking a saliva sample from your cup when you put it in the replicator and a urine sample when you were in the head. Simple, painless, and confidential. Yours, too, Captain Tiberius, although I'd like to schedule a follow-up."

Now, the captains laughed out loud. Genoa said, "Come on, Doctor. Let's get out of here before she decides to clone herself and take over our ship."

"I'm a doctor, not a pirate."

* * *

Security Officer's Log, Supplemental

My team has done a wikadas job of keeping everything running smoothly. However, just because I'm on leave does not mean I'm off duty. I got a brief overview of the changes to the systems today, and then several of my team remained to discuss "Todlie"—or "Elstodd," depending on Lieutenant Straus' mood. It's a little strange to see Lieutenant Doall so suddenly...smitten, but Straus has assured me Todd Ahndmor is "absolutely freaking adorable" and "not a threat."

Nonetheless, I've charged them with ensuring he understands the responsibilities involved when engaging in a serious relationship with our prized operations officer.

My team left giggling maniacally. A good sign.

Despite the fact that they were in port, the Impulsive cafeteria was bustling with diners. The ship had just been given the "All Clear," and people seemed to be in the mood to celebrate— or perhaps gather in large groups just to make sure a flash mob did not start. But there was no music, just the happy sound of people talking and eating, accentuated by the occasional guffaw.

Todd barely noticed. He was meeting Ellie, who had been pulled from janbot duty to help with some kind of emitter. Todd and his team had combed Communications, Second Backup for the Other Section, which was Ellie's janbot's last stop on its cleaning route, and found an odd "footprint" left by the janbot on a comms port. There wasn't any code, just the incredibly subtle presence that some form of communication had passed through that portal from a janbot. Why would janbot be transmitting anything?

A throat clearing interrupted his thoughts. He looked up.

Leslie stood at the end of the table, holding a tray with lunch. Behind her were Ensign Gel and three others, all from Security.

Leslie smiled brightly. "Are we interrupting? May we join you?"

He shrugged and indicated the empty seats. Everyone settled around him. Leslie set her tray down but then leaned over it.

"So, let me start by saying we all like you."

"Okay." He thought she meant to reassure him, but somehow, he didn't feel reassured. Possibly because, while she took the seat opposite, Gel and Sisco sat flanking him on either side, just enough in his personal space to put him on edge. The other two, a huge black guy that was all muscles and a wiry guy with a weird necklace, didn't even sit but stood behind him. Or maybe "loomed" was the better word.

"Cool." Leslie settled into her seat. "We have a saying in Security..."

"The ship is family?" Around them, other diners had surreptitiously (and less-subtly) slowed their eating and turned their chairs to better listen. He was almost glad Gel had expanded taller than his usual round self. Hopefully, the whole cafeteria wouldn't see him starting to sweat.

"Oh, good! Ellie told you. So, it's probably no surprise that we're rather protective of our shipmates, and not just for their physical safety."

"Sure, I get that. Um... are those real bones?" he asked the lanky guy, who wore a Minion's rank.

"Don't worry. I got them off the corpses."

"Oh. Okay."

"What are your intentions for Ellie?" Gel demanded.

How could something so gooey sound so hard? "Uh, you know, we've only known each other four days. Can I discuss that with her first?"

"Oh, that's a good answer. I like that answer," Leslie said. She poked at her salad and took a large bite, chewing robustly, a delighted grin on her face, while the others continued to watch him. Todd was glad the cybervirus had been eradicated, or ominous music might have started playing.

Leslie dabbed her lips with her napkin. "Yeah, you guys should really talk. But first, let us share with you our feelings about Ellie and what she means to us."

"And the ship." The deep rumbling voice had to have come from the mountain behind him.

"Tank's right. See," Leslie said, munching away at her salad with delicate enthusiasm and speaking through mouthfuls, "it's not just that we all love her because she's simply adorable. Ellie—Lieutenant Doall—is one of our most valued crewmembers."

"She saves the ship," Tank said.

Gel added, "Saves the ship, saves the mission, saves a crewman. LeRoy, how many times has she pulled some crazy miracle at the last minute?"

"Well, sir," the lanky guy answered, "I lost count after five."

Sisco said, "You've seen how Ellie's mind works. It's almost unreal."

Thinking about the past couple of days, working with her on tracking down issues with the janbots, the crazy insights, the finishing each other sentences, the sudden leaps of logic, he couldn't help but smile. "She is amazing, isn't she?"

Sisco returned his starry-eyed gaze with a scowl. "We are vested in keeping her amazing. We consider it mission-essential that she continues to be amazing."

Leslie continued, "So, speaking as people who really do like you: If you do anything to hurt Ellie…"

Gel interjected, "Or make her sad…"

Sisco added, "Or distract her in a way that keeps her from doing her best when the ship is in danger…"

Leslie shrugged, almost apologetically, "…the LT said he'd mess up your face."

Tank leaned in and said—not whispered—into his ear, "And we'll remove your spleen."

In his other ear, LeRoy added, "By way of your esophagus."

The minion's bone necklace was inches from his nose. He could see knife marks. "Okay." He cleared his throat and tried again. "Okay, because if I ever hurt her or put this ship or its mission in danger, I'd completely deserve your wrath. The ship is family, and I get how important family is. I do."

It must have been the right answer. The looming ceased. Sisco's badge chirped twice, and he tapped it twice in return. "Ellie."

"Perfect!" Leslie clapped her hands together. Then she reached out and grasped Todd's wrist like a dear friend. "I'm so glad we had a chance to talk. So, we're all still getting together for dinner and dancing, right?"

"Yeah..."

"Perfect! See you tonight!"

The men scattered, and their audience turned back to their own business. Leslie picked up her tray and headed to the recyclers. She greeted Ellie as she passed her.

Todd was still shaking his head when Ellie sat next to him. Because she was on duty, he refrained from any public display of affection, but he did move his leg to brush against hers. Her cheeks pinked, and he felt his heart leap with happiness.

"So what's going on?" she asked.

"I think I have the Impulsive Seal of Approval," he said.

* * *

Ellie paused at the cafeteria doors and scanned the room for Todd. He was at a far table, wiping his brow. He looked flustered. What could he have been doing? Could he have found some new problem?

Better to know now. She grabbed some coffee and a bagel and headed toward him.

Leslie passed by her and nudged her with her elbow. "He's a keeper," she whispered, then continued as if she'd said nothing.

What was that about? She glanced around the room. Gel. Tank. LeRoy was putting his chicken-bone necklace away. *They didn't. They wouldn't!*

Warmth vied with annoyance. She decided to ignore both and play innocent. Besides, Todd didn't look too discombobulated, so he must have fared okay. But of course, he would.

She tried to ignore the bubbling joy in her heart that the mere thought of him inspired.

"So, what's going on?" she asked as she took the seat beside him.

"I think I have the Impulsive Seal of Approval," he said, his mouth twisted in a wry grin. "The emitter check out?"

"For the most part." She set her tablet next to his and shared some code. "I mean, it's future tech from an alien world, so we really didn't want to mess with it, but I saw this, and well, a back door is a back door."

She waited while he looked over the section of code she'd shared. She loved how his brow knitted and how the world seemed to disappear for him when he concentrated. She relaxed as she watched him, enjoying the peaceful feeling she got in his presence.

Finally, he whistled. "Wow. If you hadn't pointed it out, I would not have seen it. I knew you were good with code, but—wow."

She blushed a little. "It's really because of you—because of Janbot. I don't remember all the code he taught me. I think some of it was in the nanites I was infected with. But I do remember enough that this stood out—and that's the thing. If Janbot knew it and Janbot was infected by the Cybers, then the Cybers know this code..."

"...and that means they could find and exploit it if you ever encounter them again. Yikes. You really do save the ship."

"What?"

He chuckled. "Nothing. So, what's the plan? Because I'll be honest, this is beyond me."

"Yeah, me, too. I'm passing it to up to HuFleet and Union Compusec. I think it's close enough to what Lieutenant Perez's team was doing that they'll have something for us. In the meantime, we figure the threat is low here, so we added an additional firewall and shielding. Commander Deary is setting it up with Dr. Sorcha now. I have an appointment with her in half an hour to get my brain examined, and she wants to see you, too, so we can see the emitter in action then."

"Me? What does she want to see me for?"

"She's making sure one last time that I don't have any more nanites infecting my nervous system, and she thought it'd be a good idea to check you, too." She leaned in close and whispered, "Because we've been trading so much spit."

Todd choked, making her giggle.

"Are all HuFleet ships like this?" he asked as he wiped his cheeks with one hand as if trying to rub away his embarrassment.

"The Impulsive is pretty special," she admitted.

"Then, by all means, let's do everything we can to protect it. Speaking of..."

He passed her his pad. There was an image of the comms port. It was so clean, it shined.

"This is the last thing your janbot touched on every route. Every time. Anything else gets on a schedule depending on use and level of soiling, but this is an ancillary port in a backup for a backup—this needs quarterly checks at most. Even worse, there's a twenty-nanosecond gap in the comms logs just before it cleans this item."

Ellie's eyes grew wide. "It was sending messages. For how long?"

"IT is running an algorithm to find out. We're also checking all the janbot memory cartridges we can find for memory gaps. Unfortunately, your guys did a good job slagging them."

"Yeah," Ellie sighed. "I'd say it was in the line of duty, but I think they enjoyed it, too."

From a seat two tables behind Ellie, LeRoy caught Todd's gaze. He pointed from his eyes to Todd's. He had the necklace of bones in his grip. "Yeah, your Security folks do seem to relish their job. We're going to have to check the other auxiliary communications ports as well."

"And the shuttles," Ellie said. "If any of the other janbots was also under Cyber control, they would have probably sent messages through another route. Oh, Todd, this is awful! I mean, if they got our janbots, who knows—"

"—how many other ships have been infected. Yeah, I know. My boss is loving me."

"But it's not your fault! Not any more than the teleporter accident was Dolfrick's or mine. What we have to do is make sure your boss knows you're the one to solve the problem."

"'We?'" She was so cute when she spoke first-person-plural.

Her mind was racing ahead; he didn't think she'd heard his question or his besotted tone. "We have a good start on countermeasures, but now we need to determine if they were looking for anything specific. It would be such a help if

Janbot were the first. You haven't had any other reports of janbots becoming pseudo-sentient, so... Oh! There's so much we have to tell the captain and En—the entire command staff. But first, we need to be checked that we aren't carrying any teeny spybots."

"'We'?" He'd be glad to harbor enemy nanobots, as long she kept saying "we" in that matter-of-fact way.

She leaned in and whispered, giggling, "Because of the kissing. Come on. I think you're going to enjoy meeting Dr. Sorcha in person."

"Since you helped program her, how could I not?"

They stood and left together, and if they weren't holding hands, it was only because she was on duty and her family was watching.

When Todd and Ellie entered Sickbay, Ellie stopped short at the sight of the Union medical officer speaking somewhat irately at Dr. Sorcha. Then, she saw the holoemitter band on his forearm, and things clicked. This was the emergency medical photonic technician from the UFS Scenic Route.

The Impulsive's own EMPT didn't hesitate at their arrival; in fact, she almost seemed to jump at the chance to change the subject of their discussion. "Ellie, Mr. Ahndmor. Welcome. If you'd like to take a seat, we'll begin the scans immediately. It should not take long. Would you mind if the doctor from Scenic Route observes? He'd like to do a comparative analysis of our professional methods and be available for assistance with the mobile holographic emitter."

"It's Todd, and... wow!" Todd said, looking her up and down. Then, he turned to the Scenic Route Doctor. "And you're the original version? I mean, your parameters haven't been updated?"

"Well!" the doctor replied, affronted. "Perhaps not my physical form so much, but I've been online for three years, during which time, I have made changes to my own subroutines."

Todd snickered. "That must be fun for your engineering teams. Bet your hundred-day maintenance checks are a joy."

"Hundred-day what?"

Sorcha looked at him with wry humor. "It seems captains and doctors are the worst at regular check-ups. Myself excepted, of course. My self-care routines were reinforced when Commander Deary and Lieutenant Doall—Ellie—redesigned me."

Ellie shrugged, "With everything going on with the janbots, we didn't want to take chances. Besides, Commander Deary said Simone was the cautious type."

"Simone?" the doctor asked.

"The woman we patterned Doctor Sorcha after. She was his old girlfriend. Speaking of, I thought the commander was bringing you your new emitter."

"He has. I'm using it right now."

Ellie looked at her doctor's arms, brows knit in confusion. "Where is it?"

The Scenic Route doctor replied, a sneer of distaste in his voice. "In her chest."

She added with matching asperity. "I have no need for organs, and this way, it's kept conveniently out of the way and protected from accidents. Not to mention, part of the reason for the mobile emitter is so I can do morale walks around the ship, per Ship's Sexy Directive One-C-Two-sub-b. A blocky and unattractive reminder of my artificial status diminishes my effectiveness."

The doctor crossed his arms, "And how effective are you going to be if you won't step foot outside of Sickbay?" he demanded, apparently coming back to what they'd been arguing about previously.

Dr. Sorcha met his scowl which perfectly matched his, aside for the different face and Ship's Sexy programming, "I will—once I have run it through its paces here in a secure environment. If anything goes wrong, I can quickly switch to the Sickbay emitters."

"I've been using mine just fine for three years!"

"And you do not have a 36-24-38 figure or perfect skin."

The doctor sputtered indignantly.

Taking that as agreement, Dr. Sorcha turned back to her grinning patients. "Excuse us. We've been having a professional disagreement. Please, take seats on the examining table."

With a graceful gesture, she pointed them to the interior room of Sickbay. As Todd passed, he sniffed the air. "Are you wearing perfume?"

"Yes. Thalassa's Rising. I thought as a station-dwelling Europan, you'd appreciate it. Normally, in my medical duties, I refrain from scents, but I was experimenting to see what the mobile emitter could produce. Along those lines, I'd like to conduct this examination relying on the mobile emitter as much as possible and connecting to the Impulsive for data transmission. Do you consent?"

Todd giggled like a child presented with a cool toy as he sat on the exam table. "Definitely! You're brilliant. Ellie, you're amazing. Or maybe that's vice-versa. Or both for both."

"Aw, you're so sweet!" Ellie hopped onto the table beside him. Dr. Sorcha wrapped one hand around her forearm, while the other rested on her elbow.

"But you know," Ellie said as the doctor took her blood pressure, "it might be useful to have some kind of visual indicator and external access to the holoemitter just in case there's a malfunction and one of us has to get into it."

"Your blood pressure is excellent, and hormone levels well within the expected range considering Mr. Ahndmor's presence," Dr. Sorcha replied briskly. "Open, please. That's a good idea. Do you have a suggestion?"

She stuck her finger on Ellie's tongue as her patient said, "Aaaah. A lahhlahht?"

"What are you doing?" the Scenic Route doctor exclaimed. "That's not sanitary."

"I am a photonic construct. I'm the epitome of sanitary." She scraped Ellie's cheek lightly with her fingernail. "I'll be checking your saliva and cells for nanites. A locket is an interesting idea."

Using .01 percent of her processing power, she sent out an inquiry for locket designs, modifying the search to remove anything too romantic, archaic, or sentimental, and to favor those most suited for a professional. She further narrowed parameters to metals matching her skin color and chose a size that would allow an engineer with large hands to open and flip a switch, but which would not look clunky.

Another .02 percent of her processing power synergized the design, adding a remote connection to the emitter that would allow it to reveal the actual holoemitter. While she did so, she scanned Ellie's brain for nanites, then moved to Todd, also taking his vitals and swabbing his mouth, although with the other hand, out of respect to her counterpart's sensibilities.

The locket appeared around her neck. Reaching around, Ellie gasped with delight and opened it up to see a small switch on one side and a few indicator lights on the other. "Perfect! So, how do you like the mobile emitter so far?" Ellie asked.

Dr. Sorcha pressed her fingers against Todd's neck, searching. "You have a small cyst on your thyroid. Not uncommon for someone from Europa's stations, but I want to be sure it's not nanites. Please remain still. Ellie, the photonic stability coefficient is superior. My breasts remain firm and solid."

"That's great! That will give us time to tweak the Sickbay emitters. I thought we'd have to take you down a cup size."

"That would be a shame," the Scenic Route holodoc said. "Wouldn't you agree, Mr. Ahndmor?"

"I wasn't looking!" Todd said.

Doc Sorcha replied, "Since they are right in front of you, you, in fact, were, and I told you to remain still. This is my first time conducting such a scan with this equipment. Good. Now, you'll feel a small prick, but do not hesitate to let me know if you experience other discomforts."

"What equipment?" Doctor asked.

Ellie answered, "The mobile emitter, of course. Normally, Doc Sorcha uses the Sickbay holoemitters to create the materials she needs, you know, like we do in the VR deck. Using the mobile emitter to do it is going to make things so much more efficient for away missions. Isn't that what you do?"

Doctor opened his mouth, closed it, opened it again, then frowned. "No."

"Oh, don't feel bad!" Ellie soothed. "I'm sure you've had way too much to keep you busy on the Scenic Route that you didn't have time to think of it."

Dr. Sorcha said, "Trying to cure the biota, dealing with unclassified aliens, rebuilding the medical records of a third of the crew—There are no nanites, Todd, just what's colloquially known as the Stationsider Nodules. I can remove them right now before they become a problem. Stay very still—teaching himself to sing opera. Child psychology. The art of seducing females. Stay still, Mr. Ahndmor! Now, we are done."

"Sed— Say, what?" Todd sputtered as soon as she moved her hands away.

While the holodoctor glowered, Dr. Sorcha said, "My counterpart believes that having sexual experiences helps him understand his human crewmembers. I'm interested, Todd. As a virgin, do you find your understanding of your species diminished?"

"Todd!" Ellie exclaimed with delight.

Todd shrugged shyly.

"Me, too! I just, I've been waiting for that right guy. That Forever One."

His eyes lit up. "Really? Me, too!"

"Aw! That's so sweet." She grasped his hand. If they noticed the Scenic Route doctor pinch his nose in a programmed expression of irritation, they made no indication.

After a moment in which no one needed sensors to know the hormone levels of the humans present were rising, Dr. Sorcha cleared her throat. "I've completed my examinations. You're free of any nanite infestation. I'll want you back in a month for follow up, Ellie, or before any potential encounters with the Cybers, but it's more a precaution."

"Hmm?" Ellie shook herself. "Oh! Right. Yes. Omigosh, this is such a relief. I have to talk to the captain—and Enigo. Oh, and Sorcha, go try your emitter outside. I'll bet the Captain is going to want you at the briefing, soon."

"Briefing?"

But Ellie was already tapping her comms badge and asking the captain if he had time to talk with her. "Yes, sir. It's important—but private. I mean, I don't want to get anyone's hopes up." She looked at Todd, a question in her eyes.

He smiled and made a shooing motion. "Go. Save the ship; save the mission; save the crew. I have to get with my team and track down this comms thing, anyway."

"Okay. Be ready to drop it for the briefing, though. The captain may want to talk to you, too. Oh, I'm so glad to be free of this virus!"

She hopped off the table, took two steps, then spun around and kissed his cheek. "You're so perfect," she whispered. Then she was gone.

The Scenic Route Doctor gaped at the door. "Is she always like that?"

"Hope so." Todd sighed happily, then grimaced and rubbed his neck. "Uh, should I be sore?"

"For a day or two. Take an analgesic and let me know if the soreness persists or increases. Perhaps I can pay you a house call."

"Thanks, Doc. Doctor. It was great to meet you both."

Then he was gone.

The doctor cleared his throat. "So 'house calls,' hm? Does that mean you are ready for your first foray?"

"It's the logical next step."

She changed her outfit to Ship's Sexy Workday Uniform 1, in medical green, short sleeves, no lab coat, conservative neckline, and high collar. With her hair in its professional bun, but additional make-up, she was ready for a casual walk with a coworker.

He grinned appreciatively and extended his arm. "Excellent, and while we stroll, perhaps you can explain how you are manipulating your form to work as sensor and testing equipment."

"I've already downloaded the procedures to your mainframe," she said and, ignoring his hand, sauntered out of the Sickbay.

"Of course, you have," he sighed.

* * *

Gel hesitated in front of the Botany Lab doors, feeling pressure and *déjà vu*. He hadn't wanted to have this conversation with Misha during duty hours, but Leslie had insisted he join the group for dancing, and after what Ellie had said, he couldn't wait.

I wonder if I could catch her at lunch, or maybe the gym? Someplace on neutral ground? Despite all the confidence training he'd gotten, he hated personal confrontations.

He heard an exclamation of surprise from down the hall and saw Doc Sorcha with a Union officer talking to Minion Horowitz from Life Sciences. How was she out of Sickbay? Horowitz was cooing and touching the doc's hand while Doc Sorcha said something about a mobile holographic emitter. Gel didn't know such things existed. Huh.

He briefly considered abandoning his mission and joining the group, but then he heard the LT's voice telling him to stop being a babimann. He moved toward the Botany door. It opened to admit him.

"Misha?"

"Over here."

He found her in the Carnivorous Plants section, bent over a large pot with an even larger plant with leaves the size of her head. The pod-shaped blossom bore white spines that looked a lot like teeth. It swayed sinuously. There was a circle drawn on the floor and a sign "MGM-FOS. Do not get within 3 feet."

Misha had her hands stuck in its soil up to her elbows.

The bloom lunged and snapped in Gel's direction.

Misha thocked the plant's stem with a dirty fingernail. "Odrey! Be nice. Give me just a sec, Gel. I'm almost done rotating his roots."

Odrey made a few smacking motions with its petals before settling back into its contented sway. A few moments later, Misha leaned back and smoothed the dirt over his roots. "There you go. Pulsie, light rainfall and UV290 for 15 minutes on Odrey, please."

She turned her back on the *viridi mater phaulius* and walked out of the circle.

"You have to excuse Odrey. He's a rescue and suspicious of strangers. Poor baby is really meant to be ambulatory, but his previous owner didn't take care of him, and his roots are stunted. He'd never make it in the wild. Something up?" she asked Gel. "I mean, it can't be an away mission."

Gel pulled his gaze away from the six-foot plant, which now had its blossom open to the light rain drizzling on it. There were a lot of teeth.

"Yeah, no. I just need to talk to you about something. Something Ellie said the other day. Um, do you want to clean up? I can talk while you wash."

It might be easier without her looking at him. Besides, her hands were full of dirt and some kind of goo. Did plants have sap or was it just trees?

They moved to the sink. While the running water turned the dirt into mud, he started. "The other night, when you ladies went celebrating the lieutenant's promotion."

"You can call her Ellie."

"Ellie, okay. So, I ended up walking Ellie to her room. None of us knew Todd yet, and it seemed the prudent thing..."

"Sure. It's nice how you watch out for us. All you Security, I mean."

"Right. Anyway, she said something about you, or us, or..."

Misha groaned. "Gel."

He was feeling more stupid and uncomfortable as this went on, and the sight of the mud was making him nauseous. He cut to the chase. "Look. What happened that night. I really had no idea what I was doing. It was a weird reflex, is all. I don't have any romantic feelings for you, or sexual ones, or…"

"Oh, thank heavens!"

"…I just… Wait, what?"

Misha turned toward him, her hands clean but wet. "Gel, you're a great guy. Really. But I prefer someone closer to my species."

He glopped a little in relief. "Oh, praise the Merciful Deity! So, Ellie was just drunk and full of romance. What a relief! All this time, I've been thinking you thought…"

"And I thought maybe you were, like interested…"

The two broke into laughter.

Gel handed her a towel.

"Thanks," she said, wiping her arms. "And thanks so much for coming and clearing this up. Ells and Leslie were hinting about it that night, and I thought I'd disabused them of the notion, but obviously not. I've known I should talk to you, but I could never find the right time. Guess I'm a coward."

"Considering what I just saw you doing, I would never call you a coward."

She shrugged and gazed at the damp cloth in her hands. "Taking care of plants is easy. Making friends is hard. That's why I didn't transfer right away. You know, after…"

"I really am sorry about that."

"I know. And I know space is full of crazy, unexpected stuff. Guess I'm just used to it being of the vegetative variety."

"So, friends?"

She looked up and smiled. "Yes, please."

Just then, the lab doors opened, and the holographic doctors stepped through.

The Union doctor frowned. "This isn't the arboretum."

Dr. Sorcha replied, "No. It's the botany lab. Some of the most interesting and dangerous plants are kept here for study. And why is your hand on the small of my back again?"

"Well, I—"

"You're a photonic being. It's as unnecessary as this verbal conversation you insist on."

"Doc Sorcha?" Misha exclaimed. "This is incredible. How are you out of Sickbay?"

The four quickly settled into a conversation about Doc Sorcha's experiences with the mobile holographic emitter. Gel relaxed into the peace of friendship.

Then Doc Sorcha said, "Gel, we're seeking allegorical data on a professional argument the doctor and I are having. Do you believe that engaging in sexual relations with a human would help you better understand your human crewmates?"

* * *

On the Bridge, Ellie was feeling anything but peaceful. She'd been so excited to tell the Captain about Janbot's last message to her, but now, standing in front of his ready-room door, doubt was settling in. What if it had been a ruse? What if Janbot was just trying to make her feel better, or worse yet, send the Impulsive into a trap?

A dandelion blossom floated down from above. She cupped her hands and it nestled against her palm.

Janbot sang, "Loreli! I must warn you— Loreli..."

The dandelion turned to seeds and blew away.

"Lieutenant?" Commander Smythe called from where he sat in the command chair. "Can I help you with something?"

"No, sir. Thank you, sir." She struck the door chime with a quick decisive motion. The captain had to know. He could decide what to do.

The captain sat at his desk, a big oak construction with the five-point star and an outline of Texas carved in the front. His cousin J.R. had given it to him. Near the desk was an equally archaic photo frame that she knew held a picture of him and Loreli.

The captain cocked his head, and his smile disappeared as he noted her distress. "Lieutenant? What is it?"

"Sir." She took a deep breath. "Sir, I think there might be a chance that Loreli is still somehow alive and a prisoner of the Cybers."

***

The command staff assembled in the conference room, and took seats around the barbell-shaped table. Ellie stood in the "hot seat," which was in the center of the narrow part of the table, on the side with the viewscreens. She didn't have anything on the screens today, so all eyes were on her.

Enigo was back and in uniform, as was Chief Dour. Commanders Smythe and Deary, and Ensign Sisco sat regarding Lieutenant Doall with skepticism that belied their internal struggle to believe her.

She wrung her hands with unusual anxiety. She had a hard time looking at her crewmates, especially when Enigo was grinding his teeth in an effort to keep from exploding in anger. From his seat nearest her, Todd gave her an encouraging nod.

"I'm sorry I didn't say anything earlier, but I was afraid to. With the cybersong virus, then the nanites in my head, I had no idea if they were still getting information from us. I didn't want them to know that we knew."

"That was smart, Doall," Enigo said, an automatic reply from a Chief of Security. Then the wounded man in him came through. "But it's ridiculous! Can we believe this? No offense, but that thing was manipulating you from the start, and it was in your head. It could have told you exactly what you wanted to hear."

"I don't know. Janbot didn't say anything, not even a hint, about Loreli until right before it died. I feel like it was trying to make up for what it had done. An apology."

Sisco spoke up, "All indications were that after the sweet coding Ellie did inside her own head, Janbot was cut off from any outside links. It's probably why the program faded away. Otherwise, it might have been able to get reinforcement from the cybersong virus affecting the ship."

"Or," Enigo countered, "it was programmed all along to set a trap and used its last words to finish its mission."

Ellie looked miserable with doubt. Jeb knew exactly how she felt. All eyes turned to him, seeking direction, if only for the next step in the discussion, but he found his brain frozen, reliving those horrifying few minutes:

Dour over the comms, sounding young and afraid. "The beams. We crossed the beams."

Deary said, "It was the tumble, Captain. We hadn't received all the data, and when the beam looped in on itself... We're facing cascading intermixing of the photonic matrix. If we materialize them, every molecule in their body will explode at the speed of light."

"Put them back in the buffer," Jeb ordered.

"We can't. The streams have become too complex. The consoles are supercharging. Get out of here, the lot of you, and close the blast door behind you. It's been an honor."

"Doall?" Jeb asked. He'd give his ops officer one last chance to pull a miracle, then he was dragging both officers away by their ears if need be.

Ellie sobbed. "Send them back."

"What?" Enigo roared. "There's no planet there."

"It doesn't matter. The data stream is too confused. Chief, reverse the matter stream."

"No!" Enigo exclaimed. "No, for the love of God..."

Ellie pleaded to the captain with her eyes.

The Impulsive counted eight seconds to their destruction.

Jeb spoke the words that would haunt him the rest of his life. "Chief, do it."

Could Loreli really be alive, a prisoner of the Cybers? Oh, Sprout!

Commander Smythe broke the silence. "Did Janbot give any details? How it happened, where she might be?"

Ellie shook her head. "No. Just that she's alive and the Cybers have her hostage."

Smythe nodded. "Cybers don't take hostages. They destroy and integrate the pieces they find useful. I must agree with Lieutenant LaFuentes. It sounds like a trap, at least in intention."

Jeb pursed his lips, then shook his head. "I'm not so sure. If they meant it as a trap, and for the janbot to send us there, it would have given a few more clues, not just a cryptic warning."

Enigo was rubbing his knuckles as if reminding himself that the last time he lost his temper, he broke his fist on a wall. He looked from Ellie to Dour to Commander Deary. "Much as I hate to say this, how could this even be possible? You said the teleporter streams had crossed. You said the data was a complete jumble. We sent them back to a planet that didn't even exist anymore. So how could she be alive? And what about the Doc? Did your janbot Romeo mention him?"

Ellie slumped into the chair beside Todd. "No. Just Loreli. But he only had a fragment of a verse to warn me before he faded. Maybe he couldn't fit the doctor in?"

Suddenly, Dolfrick looked up, his eyes shining with dark, brooding intelligence. "The Cybers would have the capability to untangle the streams. If they intercepted the signal we sent back…"

Ellie gasped. "The KatHack program! Loreli was probably carrying it. It seemed to trust her."

Todd said, "The what?"

"The KatHack program. Kuricrearrogance. That was the whole reason the Cybers were at Filedise. They had come to pick up the program, but it had become sentient and didn't want to go. Loreli and the doctor were teleporting up with the only copy."

"How would they know?" Jeb asked. "They would have had to have known we were reversing the signal."

"Janbot!" Ellie sat up. "He was there, Captain, in auxiliary control. I didn't think anything of it at the time, with so much going on, but would it matter? All the ships were destroyed in the explosion and the fight."

"Were they?" Enigo tapped the table before him, and a replica of the security console came up. His fingers raced over the keyboard, pulling up the sensor logs of that day. They waited.

"We missed one," he murmured, then with a laugh that may have masked a manly sob, he said, "We missed one! Keptar's cheek, Captain! She could be alive."

Jeb held up a hand, as much to calm his own excitement as that of his people. "It's an incredible longshot, and we don't have enough information to do anything about it, anyway. We're a HuFleet ship, and we can't go haring off on a wild goose chase, even if it is for one of our own.

"I want information and a plan I can take to HuFleet Command. If you need someone in particular, discuss it with Commander Smythe and Doc Sorcha. Let's respect shore leaves as much as possible. I want a 12-hour recall window on anyone leaving the station, but otherwise, if we don't have to have them here, let them go. We're not going to rush this. If they have our people—and it's a big 'if'—then we need to be at our best if we're going to get them back."

He turned to Dolfrick, "Chief, you feeling up to returning to duty?" It was a formality since Dr. Sorcha had cleared him that morning.

"I am eager to return to the arms of my mistress and coax her to reveal her secrets to me. If indeed, the Cybers tasted of her virtues, I shall uncover it."

Translation: *I want to figure out how the Cybers hijacked the teleporter streams.*

"Welcome back, Chief. However, I understand from your sister that you're helping her with a show she wants to put on for the crew. You make time for family, got it? Same for you, Lieutenant LaFuentes."

With a chorus of "aye, sir"s, the briefing broke up and everyone went their ways. When the others had left, Phineas rose, squeezed Jeb's shoulder, and headed to the bridge.

Jeb turned to the window. It faced away from the station, and without the need for shields or the interference of speed to blur the objects of space, the screens showed the actual starry skies. Without a sextant (a highly technical device that held the star charts of the mapped universe along with directional tools), he couldn't tell which way lay the ruins of Filedise.

Not that it mattered; the Cyber ship had had weeks to travel. It could be anywhere.

Please, he prayed. There was no grabbing of his butt, no appeals to Keptar. Just the raw cries of his heart. Please, let it be true and keep her safe 'till we get her back.

We'll find you, Sprout. I swear.

* * *

Phineas rang the chime to Jeb's quarters and entered when invited. In the crook of his arm balanced an old-fashioned picnic basket with a big red bow. A querulous meow issued from it. One of Chief Loggins' minions had been on his way to deliver it, but Phineas intercepted him and took on the chore. He knew why Jeb had sent the logistics officer after a katt and whom it was for.

He found his CO and best friend leaning toward the mirror, carefully trimming his beard. Earlier that day, he'd used a follicle stimulator to quick-grow a rugged five o'clock shadow. He wore polished cowboy boots, tight jeans, and a button-down shirt. The buttons were pearl snaps that matched the collar tabs. On the counter beside him was his cowboy hat.

Phineas sighed. He thought Jeb had gotten over her seven years ago.

"She knows about the hat, you know."

Jeb frowned as he regarded the tan Stetson. When he wasn't in Texas, he generally only wore it when riding, when he needed to display his ethnic heritage, or when he was hoping a beautiful woman would give him a reason to remove it.

"I thought you gave up on Katika after she married your cousin."

"She ain't married to him anymore," Jeb said, "and she invited me to dinner—and you'll note you were not included in the invitation. Still, point taken."

Jeb opened the basket and reached in to caress the silky fur of the katt. "Hey, Loggie found one!"

Katts, for those who have not read earlier stories or who have forgotten, are genetically engineered small mammals designed specifically for life aboard starships. They have the amiability and desire to please of dogs but the independent nature of cats. Skilled predators with stomachs of steel, they wander the vents and nooks looking for vermin that inevitably end up on a ship despite the best screenings, but they are also up for cuddles and instinctively sense when a crewman needs purr therapy. One of the best things about katts, however, is that they "go" only in their kattboxes.

Jeb had given Katika a katt when she took command of the Scenic Route, but she'd told them Claws II had died in the mu quadrant. He'd immediately asked Chief Loggins to find another.

Looking at the grin on Jeb's face as he scratched the kitten's ears made Phineas want to sigh again. "Just don't expect too much? There's one sure way to know if a woman wants to be kissed."

Jeb rolled his eyes. "I remember your trick."

"It's not a trick. It's subtlety. It's romantic. And it works."

Jeb chuckled with fond exasperation as he tucked the katt back into the basket. "All right. I'll remember. And if she just wants a platonic dinner with an old friend, I'm okay with that. I'm just glad to see her back safe."

Phineas had his doubts, but when they exited together, Jeb left his hat behind.

* * *

The UFS Scenic Route was a sleek vessel built to explore uncharted deep space for extended periods without encountering a Union station or habitable world. Thus, it had been designed for scientific operations and for luxurious hominess to keep the crew comfortable during extended time between star systems. It had not, however, been designed for five years in often hostile territory. Every scorch mark and replaced panel was a testimony to the grit of the crew and the leadership of their captain. Even so, the Scenic Route would still be in drydock undergoing repairs long after the Impulsive was back on duty.

Still, Jeb had to admire the wide, windowed halls and soft carpet that muffled the sound of his boots as he made his way to the captain's quarters.

Don't get yer hopes up, he reminded himself as he took a breath, checked the tuck of his shirt, and rang the chime.

Kat opened the door wearing a loose, peach-colored silk shirt and matching pants. Her hair was down and her make-up definitely not at her usual conservative level.

His grin grew as wide as his eyes. "Well, howdy, ma'am!"

She laughed and looked him over carefully. "Howdy yourself. No hat?"

He was suddenly glad he'd taken Phin's advice. He would've come off as too eager. "I wasn't sure what kind of dinner this was," he said.

"Oh. You've gotten wiser since we last saw each other. Come in." She backed up to let him enter, then pointed at the basket. "For me?"

He handed it to her, careful not to let their hands touch, enjoying the anticipation as well as the instant camaraderie. "I know you prefer dogs, but..."

"No ship should be without a katt," they finished together.

"Oh, Jeb. He's darling!" She reached in and picked up the katt, cuddling him close and scratching it behind the ears. He bumped his head under her chin. "And you were right about a ship needing a katt. Claws II certainly earned his keep, and not just in comforting the crew. He actually saved the crew once."

"Serious?"

"Mm-hmm. We were being experimented on by hyper-intelligent pan-dimensional beings. We had no idea, but they were trying different experiments on each of us. I had a migraine for three weeks. My first officer went prematurely gray. Two of my crew couldn't keep their hands off each other… Anyway, we had no idea what was going on until 'Two left a dead little rodent on my pillow. The next day, he left another one. After the fifth one, my headaches were gone, and people started getting back to normal.

"By this time, we'd been through enough that we were not going to assume we had a mouse infestation, so we did a closer examination and discovered the 'mice' were a protrusion into our dimension of the scientists doing the experiments. You should be getting a sensor update with their dimensional frequency, just in case they start making inroads to our section of space. In the meantime, keep an eye out for white mice. Little white mice—it makes an odd kind of sense, doesn't it?"

As she spoke, she made her way to the replicator. Jeb followed.

Still snuggling her newest crew member, she told the replicator, "Feline supplement 129, a bowl of water, and a temporary kattbox."

Jeb helped her put the things in a corner, and she set down the katt in front of the bowl, where it ate tidily. She ran two fingers along its back, making it arch.

"Thank you. He's beautiful."

"You're beautiful."

Still stroking the katt, she turned her head to cock a brow at him.

"Seriously, you are. I didn't expect to see you dressed so... I thought you might be..." He shrugged.

She stood, and brushed off her blouse, a dog-lover's habit, since katts did not shed. She ordered a couple of drinks and handed him one. "Jeb. I got over Grant three years and four lovers ago."

He almost choked on his drink. "Lovers? You?"

Now she laughed and led them to the couch. They sat apart but facing each other. "I know, I know. I was always so focused. But after Grant, and with all the stress of our predicament and the many, many attractive males in the mu quadrant... It just didn't make sense anymore."

She studied her glass as she spoke, running one finger along its rim. "It's funny, in a way. Grant and I knew this was a five-year command. After that, I was going to retire, take a civilian job, start a family. When we got trapped in the mu quadrant, I told myself, I'd give it five years—the length of the mission. If at that point, we were no closer to finding a way home, I'd let him go. I could give us five years.

"Apparently, Grant couldn't. Not even a year."

"And you came home a week before your five-year mission was up. I told him he was an idiot."

She nodded to herself. "Just as well. Despite everything, I love command. I don't think I would have given it up."

She met Jeb's gaze. "Tell me: Is he happy? Did he marry that Derulian?"

"Yeah. They have two kids."

"Good. I don't think we'd have made it through the stress of my command under a normal tour. And now, after all I've been through..." Her lips quirked in a sad, rueful grin, and she changed the subject. "What about you? How are you holding up after losing Loreli?"

He blinked at the change of subject, but the news of the morning filled his heart with cautious optimism. "She might be alive, after all."

"What?" Kat set her glass down with a thunk and half-stood. "Where? Let's go!"

He grabbed her arm and gently pulled her back down. "Hold on, there! I thought I was the captain of the Impulsive. We're not ready to act yet."

Her eyes flashed. "You know I loved that sprout like she was my own child. If there's any way I or my ship can help, we're in."

"I know," he said, gratitude and warmth flowing in his voice. He couldn't help thinking how fun it would be to go on a mission together, too. The Cybers wouldn't know what hit them. "Right now, all we have is a cryptic warning from a malfunctioning janbot. My people are working out if it's even possible, and if so, where we can find her and how we can get her back."

"If you need anything, we're at your disposal," she said.

"I'll let you know."

He was still touching her arm. She set her hand over his. "Promise me."

He'd forgotten how deeply blue her eyes were. "I promise."

They fell silent then, both too full of things they wanted to say, none of them appropriate for the moment.

Then she started to trace lazy circles on the back of his hand with her finger. It sent tingles up his arm, headier than the wine he hadn't drunk.

"So," he drawled, "what kind of dinner were you thinking, then? Should I go back and get my hat?"

She smiled, her gaze still on his hand, her fingers moving meditatively. "I'm tempted. I have been since we saw each other yesterday. But... I need a friend. Someone who understands me and my position, someone I can talk to, captain-to-captain. I think maybe you could use one, too? Maybe we should play it by ear."

She looked up as he sucked in a breath. "What?"

He grimaced. "Sorry. Just an unfortunate choice of words, considering what my ship has been through with the cybersong virus."

She snickered, and then they were both laughing. "I'm sorry! Yes, that must have been torture for you. You're as tone deaf as I am!"

He wagged a finger at her. "Ah, but now I have the advantage. I've had two weeks of having my brain rewired."

"Oh, so you can carry a tune?"

"I didn't say that, exactly. But I might just be able to play it by ear for a while."

He threaded his fingers between hers. "And no matter where this leads, I've always been and will always be your friend."

They spent the night talking, snacking, drinking. They named the katt, "Claws III" or "Tre" for short. Five years of hardships and joys, regrets and reassurances... They barely scratched the surface of it all, but it was enough.

When the clock called them back to their respective ships, Jeb reached out and caressed her hair, and when she seemed fine with that subtle gesture, he kissed her.

* * *

Todd had long since progressed from touching Ellie's hair, and she was perfectly okay with that. In fact, every caress, every touch of his lips made her hunger for more. And when his hands strayed from the small of her back to the hem of her miniskirt, Oh, Keptar!

"What does that even mean, anyway?" he asked as he nibbled her ear.

"Hm?" Then her brain caught up to what she'd said. She broke away laughing. "Oh, no! Please, never, never tell anyone I say that!"

"Okay," he said amiably enough, but there was a question in his tone.

Grinning with embarrassment, she explained about the captain's new religion of Keptarianism, and how the squeezing of the butt cheeks was a blessing. "If he ever finds out I say that, I don't know if he'd think I'm a blasphemer or a convert."

"You guys encounter the weirdest stuff." Todd leaned back against the couch, shaking his head.

He was so cute with that bemused grin and his hair all rumpled. She did so love how silky his hair felt. He was so much more than cute, though. He was kind and insightful and wikadas intelligent and… and…

…and she loved him.

His brows knit. "What's wrong? You look like your brain's being hijacked. Are you hearing Janbot?"

"What? No! No, I…" Her mind scrambled to come up with a reasonable cover. "I just realized what time it is. I need to change if we're going dancing. I'll be right back."

He frowned, not quite believing. "Are you sure you're okay?"

"I promise. The only one on my brain is you." She stood, then kissed him gently on the lips. They were so soft and perfect. She pushed away quickly. If she stayed, she'd confess her feelings. She shut the door to her room, tossed off her uniform, then went to the sink and splashed cold water on her face. Oh, Keptar!

They'd only met four days ago. They couldn't possibly know each other well enough. She always took the slow road in relationships. This wasn't like her.

And yet, it was.

She braced her arms on the sink and leaned in toward her reflection. "Get it together, Doall.

Loreli is still out there, and we need to find her, and Enigo will break Todd's beautiful face if I let him distract me. There's time enough to figure out later if this is infatuation or..."

She looked away and stifled a giggle. Who was she kidding? She was so in love!

Time for that later. We have a job to do. Besides, who knows if he feels the same.

It may interest the reader to know that, while he replicated snacks and drinks, Todd was having nearly the same conversation with himself.

Thus, when Ellie emerged dressed in a twirly but not-too-flashy dress for dancing, they were both completely aware that they were staring into the eyes of their perfect match, but they each silently resolved to stay professional and not let the other know.

They stood apart, suddenly shy.

Todd studied the empty table as he struggled to regain his focus. "Um, so I was thinking."

She gave a little start. "Oh?"

"About Janbot, I mean."

"Oh. Okay. So...?"

"If we knew what it was sending the Cybers, it might help to find Loreli, but the transmissions were too quick and most likely encrypted."

"Then we have to surmise what it might have sent. Maybe if we look at what was happening around it on its route. We could compare it to the duty logs."

She went to her desk. Todd followed. He pulled one of the chairs beside her.

* * *

Jeb sauntered back to the Impulsive in the middle of the night shift. Since they were in port, that meant there was only a skeleton crew, and most everyone else was sleeping or enjoying their off time. The corridors were empty. Which was just as well; Jeb knew he was wearing an expression his momma would have called "twitterpated."

He didn't care. It had taken eight years, but he'd finally gotten the kiss he'd dreamed about since he'd first laid eyes on a spunky redhead ensign who'd been assigned to show Phin and him around their first assignment.

His quarters were not far from the bridge, as was the tradition for all human ships, but he didn't make a side trip to check on things.

Instead, he went straight to his quarters, plopped into a chair, and put his feet on the table. He leaned his head back and relived that first kiss, letting himself bask in the happiness. Loreli might be alive, and Kati like-liked him. He hadn't felt this hopeful in a long time. He wanted to savor it before something came along to mess it up.

The doorbell chimed.

Thinking it was Phin wanting a report on his date, he hustled to the door. Phin was there, but so were Lieutenant Doall and Todd Ahndmor. They all looked grim.

And there it is, he thought.

"Come on in and tell me about it," he said. As they settled at the table, he replicated a pot of coffee and four cups. He'd been sailing on endorphins—and other happy hormones—but the others looked weary.

Ellie accepted her cup, then began, "You see, sir, we got to thinking about Janbot, and what exactly he might be reporting to the Cybers, and why he was in auxiliary control the day... of the crisis." Even now, she hesitated to say, "the day Loreli and the doctor were killed."

Todd took up the narrative. "It turns out it was a complete coincidence. It was just Janbot's regular day, and when the battle started, it stayed to pass on intel."

Ellie cut in, "But there was so much comms traffic, it hid what he was doing."

Jeb nodded. The Cybers had been unusually chatty.

Ellie continued. "So we think there was a connection between the Cybers and Janbot right when the teleportation was failing. Remember that weird message I got? 'Behind you?' I didn't know what it meant, and then so much happened I forgot about it, and later after the weirdness of Janbot, I thought it might have been a message just to say he was there as support—"

"—but this was before it started getting weird and emotional—" Todd interjected.

"—so we thought, 'What if it was KatHack?' You know, the kuricrearrogance program? Well, if that was the case, then it could very well have been part of the cybervirus that infected the ship."

"So it wasn't from the replicator virus?"

For readers who have forgotten or missed some episodes—shame on you! Go back to Season 1, do not pass Go!—a virus started causing the replicators to produce all manner of odd products.

"Exactly, sir. Which is why we were the only ship infected with the cybersong virus."

"Interesting, but not worth a two-a.m. briefing," Jeb said. He wasn't chiding so much as saying he was ready for the really bad news.

"No, sir. As you recall, the first outbreaks of song happened a day or two after the crisis at Filedise. We checked the visual records, and Janbot started reporting to the Cybers every day after that," Ellie started.

Todd passed over a tablet. "Even worse, it changed its maintenance routine without logging the differences."

The tablet projected a 3-dimensional map of the ship. Janbot's route zigged-zagged all over it, with dots of varying sizes to show stops—the larger the circle, the longer it lingered. At each stop were music notes to indicate song.

"So, it was influencing us to make music?"

Ellie said, "More likely, it was listening—and analyzing."

Jeb leaned back and swore. Music was one of the main weapons biological beings had against the Cybers. The creative, emotional aspects confused their logical pathways.

"Yes, sir. With even part of the KatHack now incorporated into its programming, it could understand song and pass that understanding to the Cybers. But it gets worse."

She expanded a part of the holographic schematic to the crew quarters, then to a single room. "This is Lieutenant LaFuentes' room."

Jeb rubbed his forehead. "Had he been listening to Dread Oog Rage Metal?"

There are two forms of music known to be dangerous to most humanoid life forms. First, the orchestral compositions of the Logic B'Lather, which are so mind-numbingly complex they could knock out most intelligent life forms. (For the rest, they became incessant earworms.) Then, there was Dread Oog Rage Metal.

While the originating species classified it as "smooth jazz," the effect on the humanoid brain was to overload the fight and flight responses to the point of suicidally murderous frenzy. It had a similar effect on artificial intelligences. The inhabitants of the UGS Hood, Enigo's home, had been subjected to it at a young age and could not only tolerate it but also embraced it as part of their heritage.

"Most likely, sir. All the sensing equipment was off in his room many of the times Janbot tarried there. It's noted in the logs, but no one thought anything about it since, well, he was grieving."

Todd said, "But Janbot, with the KatHack program infecting his system, could have adapted to the music—and then passed that adaptation on to the Cybers."

"Hellfire." Jeb sat back, thinking. Enigo had used Dread Oog Rage Metal to destroy the Cyber ships at Filedise. It had been spectacularly effective. Now, they'd not only have a defense against it, but most likely, they knew the effect it had on Union ships and their "biological components."

He turned to Smythe. "We send out a report to the fleet?"

Smythe nodded, "Yes, Captain, and to Union Central."

"All right, that's the best we can do for the moment. Tomorrow, I want people thinking about how we deal with this threat. Ah!" He held up a warning finger at Ellie and Todd, who had leaned forward as one to share their ideas. "I said, 'Tomorrow.' If you had a cure-all, you'd have led with that, so since we aren't fixing this now, a good night's sleep won't hurt. Now, go on. Commander, if you'd stay a spell?"

When the others left, Jeb gave his friend a rueful grin. "It just never stops, does it?"

"Apparently not."

He pointed toward the door with his thumb. "Have those two been finishing each other's sentences all night?"

Phineas relaxed in the chair. "Apparently so. Lieutenant Straus has started a ship's pool concerning their engagement."

"We're leaving day after tomorrow..." He looked to the ceiling. "Pulsie, put me down for tomorrow evening at nine o'clock, he'll pop the question."

"And how was your evening?" Phineas asked.

Jeb's grin said it all, but that didn't stop them from talking about it for the next hour.

* * *

Ellie and Todd walked down the corridor. Since it was empty, and she wasn't in uniform, he reached out to take her hand. She squeezed it, smiling. It made his heart skip, and yet…

"The captain seemed really concerned," he said.

Her smile slipped just a little. "Well, music has been an advantage. The Cybers have never processed it well. But don't worry. We'll come up with something. We're HuFleet. We're spunky and innovative."

When they entered the lazivator and its doors closed, he leaned against the wall with an exaggerated groan. "How do you do it?"

"Do what?"

"It's two in the morning. I think we've had six hours' sleep in the last forty-eight. My brain is mush."

She giggled. "Oh, my poor Toddybear."

He ignored her to continue whining, "And my feet hurt, and my legs feel like we're in heavy gravity. I don't want to walk back to my hotel room."

"So don't. Stay with me. My couch is plenty comfy."

"Won't people talk?"

She snuggled against his arm. "Pulsie can vouch for us. I'm sure there's a betting pool going on. It's important to be accurate."

"On your virginity? Your ship is so weird." But he let her walk him back to her quarters, get him a pillow and blanket, and tuck him in with a kiss.

He closed his eyes and dozed.

Later, he woke up and tiptoed to her door. He peeked in. She was curled up in her sheets, hugging a pillow, sound asleep. A katt was snuggled against her knees. He opened one eye to peer at Todd, then dismissed him as not a threat.

Todd crept back to the living room, turned on Ellie's computer, and pulled up the ship's records of the Impulsive's past fights against the Cybers.

* * *

Todd awoke to the smell of hot coffee and someone poking him on the shoulder. He rolled over to blink blearily at a perky and made-up Ellie. He glanced at the chronometer. 0800

"How long have you been up?"

"A couple of hours. You were sleeping so soundly. I went to the bridge to get some things organized for our leaving tomorrow, then came back to see if you wanted breakfast before our last janbot briefing. I also replicated you some fresh clothes."

"You're amazing!" He snagged the outfit folded on the table and ducked into the bathroom for a quick shower. When he returned, she'd laid out a standard Europan breakfast of muffins and poached eggs on a bed of kale. He dug in, but she watched him, chin resting in her hand.

"Did you learn what you needed to last night?"

A protest of ignorance rose to his lips, but she looked at him with seriousness, yet no scolding. He set his fork down. "How'd you know?"

"Pulsie told me. I'm not mad. Pulsie would never have let you see classified information. Those logs were need-to-know, and you needed to know. So...?"

"Music wasn't just an advantage. It was *the* advantage. It played a decisive role in every victory."

She shrugged. "We were getting into a rut. We'll find another strategy."

"Because you're spunky and innovative?"

She grasped his arm. "Because we have too much to protect."

Their eyes met. The silence filled with the words they wanted to say.

Finally, Todd dared to voice them. "Ell, there's something I've been wanting to say, and I know it's crazy—"

"Omigosh! Me, too!"

His heart leaped joyfully. Their words tumbled over the others:

"Really? Because it seems too soon."

"It's only been five days."

"But every moment has been so..."

"And I've never felt like this!"

"I can't let you leave..."

"I can't go without you knowing..."

They finished in unison: "I love you!"

They paused, absorbing what just happened. Then they broke out into giggles.

Ellie gasped, "The time!"

They snatched last bites of muffin and dashed out.

When the coast was clear, Pipes, the ship's katt, slinked out of the bedroom and hopped on the table to finish the eggs.

* * *

Todd didn't know how he managed to act normal when he was swimming in a sea of light and joy. Ellie loved him! But somehow, he managed to make his way through the outbriefing, giving his presentation to the main officers of the Impulsive and the HuFleet and Union admirals who had teleconferenced in. His own boss was there, as was Keh Renn from Legal. His mouth moved on automatic while he concentrated on not blushing and keeping a serious expression. All seemed pleased at whatever he said, but he didn't remember a word of it.

Afterwards, Commander Smythe and Captain Tiberius pulled Ellie aside, so he waited by the door.

Commander Smythe told her, "Ensign Smirnov needs some leadership experience. I'd like him to handle preparing Ops for our departure. Ensure he knows what needs to be done. Mr. Ahndmor can wait for you here."

How she could say "Yes, sir," with such aplomb baffled him and made him love her more. When she left through the door to the bridge, the two men turned to him.

"Have a seat," the captain said.

He did so, smirking, "Just so you know, Security has already said what they'd do to me if I ever hurt Ellie."

The two officers exchanged glances.

"Were you going to threaten bodily harm?" the captain asked his first officer.

Smythe replied, "I wouldn't think it necessary or appropriate."

Todd felt his face redden. "I'm sorry! I thought… Is this about the janbots?"

"Oh, no. This is about our lieutenant," the captain replied. "We just want to be sure you understand what you're getting into."

He gulped. "Sir?" He thought he'd be having this conversation with her father. Somehow that seemed less intimidating.

Smythe steepled his fingers. "Lieutenant Doall is the amazing officer—the amazing woman—that she is, not just because of her genius and ability to think outside the box. She's driven."

"Loyal and dedicated," the captain added.

"And has an insatiable need to be useful on a grand scale. She won't be happy with anything less. If you want a relationship with her, you'd better be ready for all that implies."

"Absolutely, sir!" But what did it imply?

These were not the people to ask.

Before he could figure out what else to say, Ellie stepped into the briefing room. "He's all set, sir, Captain," she told them as she moved to take a seat by Todd. She gave him a curious glance. "Did you want us to work on the Cyber issue, Captain?"

He waved toward the door. "I don't think I can stop you from working on it but do so in the backs of your minds. I want you to take a day off."

"Sir?"

Todd saw how her brow knit just slightly in confusion, and how she stiffened, as if about to protest. The captain's advice hit home.

But the captain pointed at the door. "Git. Just don't forget the variety show tonight."

"No, sir! Of course not, sir. Thank you!"

Once the door closed behind Ellie and him, she let out a squeak of joy. "Is there anything you have to do today?"

"I have to pack, and I promised I'd bring home souvenirs. Shoot! I was going to ask the

Captain to sign something for my little brother. He's crazy about starship captains. He collects the cards."

"That's easy. We can ask after the pageant. Let's replicate one for Captain Genoa, too. Who else?"

"That's the problem. Mom's a freighter captain. She's got a pretty steady route, but when she goes someplace new, she always brings back something cool. I never go anywhere, so I have to outdo her." While he told her about the other siblings at home expecting trinkets, they made their way to the lazivator.

Meanwhile, Jeb and Phineas went to the Bridge.

"Do you think he understood what we were saying?" Phin asked.

"He'd better have, 'cause if he hurts her, I'll kick his butt," Jeb answered.

* * *

Misha looked up from a plant she was misting and smiled at Ellie and Todd as they entered the botany ward. "Hey, you two! Where were you last night? Never mind! I don't need to know. You missed a lot of fun, though. Gel is a weirdly good dancer."

Ellie smiled, "So you made up?"

Misha held up both hands to forestall any jumped conclusions. "We're just friends, El. That's all we ever were and all we'll ever be. Neither of us is into that level of species variance. What brings you here? Fyodor said you put him in charge of preparations. He's so bossy."

"Todd has a little brother who's interested in botany, and he wants to bring him home something special. I thought maybe...?"

"Hmm." Misha frowned. "How interested is he?"

Soon Misha had gifted him with a small pot holding the cutting of a Primeval Hisser of Juras 2. The thick-leaved plant earned its name because it responded to sudden, near movement by rearing back and hissing. "It's completely harmless, but it looks cool," Misha reassured him. Plus, it pulled moisture and nutrients from the air, making it easy to care for.

"But if your brother follows the instructions, this little cutting will be ready to bloom just about the time he's going to want to impress girls," Misha concluded.

"What's next?" Ellie asked.

"I'm getting Raela candy that's spun in vacuum, but I'll do that tomorrow."

They entered the lazivator, where they had spent many joyful minutes, talking, holding hands on the sly, and a time—or twenty—stopping it altogether for a real kiss. He was going to miss that lazivator.

Ellie broke his thoughts. "What about your parents? Don't they get anything?"

"I was thinking about that," he said, which was a complete lie. His mouth was moving on automatic, while a tiny part of his superego was shouting, "Don't do it! Think about what the captain said! It's too soon!"

But Ellie was there, and she was so wonderful, and his heart was so full. The words tumbled out.

"I thought, maybe, they'd like a future daughter-in-law?"

Her eyes got wide. "Pulsie! Stop the lazivator!" She set her hands over his. "Toddy, are you sure? I mean, there's so much we don't know about each other, and so much to consider…"

Of course, she'd be thinking that. Could she be any more perfect? "I don't care. I know we'll make it work. I love you."

"I love you, too. And yes, omigosh, yes. I'll marry you."

* * *

With the Impulsive and the Scenic Route crews attending, the variety show had been moved to the largest cargo bay on the station, but you couldn't tell from looking at it. Gloria Joy had insisted on creating a comfortable but unique experience, and what Gloria Joy Dour wanted, Gloria Joy Dour got.

So, rather than an indoor theater, the bay had been made up as an outdoor amphitheater, with holographic blue skies and a simple stage surrounded 180 degrees by elevated bench seating. These were all replicated by her own proprietary design. The seats looked like rock, but were in fact, amazingly comfortable. The stage was set at the perfect distance and height that everyone got a good view, and Gloria Joy had made Dolfrick wander around the stage reciting his poetry while she tweaked the acoustic plating around the bay.

As a result, anything from the stage could be heard with perfect clarity, while the noise of the waiting crowd was just a dim background hum. The seating split rather evenly between the two crews, with the Impulsive security team claiming a central section from which to cheer their LT.

Ellie and Todd sat in seats in front of them. Ellie was turned around in her seat so she could show Leslie and Gel her engagement ring. After her acceptance, she and Todd had gone back to her room so they could design it together. Rather than a large diamond, still a traditional choice among humans, hers held 45 small citrine chips in the shape of a dandelion bloom.

In the front row, Jeb pretended to mope a little about losing the ship's pool, telling Phin it was all their fault for giving her the day off. Then, the doors opened, and instinct made him look up. Captain Kat Genoa headed his way. She wore tight jeans and a loose, low-cut blouse and somehow, Jeb thought she looked even better than she had the night before. He was so glad he was wearing his hat, despite Phin's warnings that it was rude to wear in a theater.

When she got to the pair, she eyed the Stetson, then with a frown of mock disapproval, whipped it off his head. She spun it between her fingers, then settled it onto her lap as she sat down. Then, she turned away from him to talk to her crewmen. Todd leaned forward to ask her to sign a collector's card, and she asked about his brother and cooed over Ellie's ring.

Jeb forced his face into something resembling neutrality, but he knew he was as smitten as his ops officer. When the sky started to darken and take on the pinks of sunset, he slipped his hand onto her leg under the hat. She gave him a sidelong glance and a smirk, but otherwise, pretended not to notice.

Toward the top of the amphitheater, the holographic doctors sat together. The Scenic Route doctor was pointing things out and Doc Sorcha was letting him while she did her own observations, because she'd concluded that he was not going to give up his analog prattling around her. Sorcha was running Ship's Sexy Casual Evening Program 3, and the Scenic Route holodoc was preening like he'd won the lottery.

Seeing Jeb's casual flirtation, the doctor decided to imitate the gesture and put his hand on Sorcha's thigh. Without turning her attention from the crowd, she set a hand over his and disrupted his holoemission to halfway up his arm. He yanked his arm away, giving her a shocked, dirty look that she ignored.

The stage lit up, the spotlight on Gloria Joy. She welcomed everyone and introduced the first act, a chorus of popular songs from the Sol system.

For the next hour, people clapped, laughed, and cheered for the performers—and Dolfrick, whenever anyone caught the black-clad teleporter chief moving a piece of the stage. If they could not see his glare, they felt it, which only encouraged some of the Impulsive crew to cheer harder. Jeb whistled through his fingers for the baton twirler. The flashing metal tube and tasseled white boots took him back to his high school marching band days.

Then, Gloria Joy came out to introduce the last act before the final chorus.

"We have seen representations of cultures across our section of space, but there's one culture that has always been a mystery. When most people think of the UGS Hood, they think only of violence and division. They have been shunned as a ship and respected individually only for those warlike traits that have defined them for generations.

"But as I have come to know more about these people through my friendship with Marisol and her parents, I have seen so much more. Loyalty. Intelligence. Compassion. And hope! Oh, so much hope soaring from a history of grief. There is no better way to express that than in music. But first—we must travel to the UGS Hood!"

She spread her arms, and suddenly, the room began to change. The twilight sky and grassy knoll became hard, metal bulkheads. The stage transformed into a knotwork of pipes. Nestled into them was Enigo. He wore brown leather pants (actually, Dread Oog hide, a detail Gloria Joy tactfully omitted). His shirt was two strips of brightly patterned material that crisscrossed in the back and hung loosely over his chest, weighted down by metallic lace. He cradled his guitar.

Minion Jenkins started to whoop and was quickly silenced by his peers. Enigo had made it clear that if anyone took the focus off his chica, the entire Security Staff would be running laps on the hull.

When Marisol came out, also in hide pants, but with a blouse full of flounces and a train, the crowd went appropriately wild. Enigo silenced them with a strum that echoed off the artificial bulkheads. He played an introduction, then Marisol took over with the trumpet.

The notes poured out, strong and energetic, too wild to be martial but with the same effect of stirring the blood. Security from both ships whooped approval.

But then the melody slowed, growing haunting and anguished. The crowd grew silent, each person in the audience remembering a lost comrade, an opportunity missed, a regret not resolved.

Jeb heard sniffles behind him. Ellie, or maybe Leslie Straus. He glanced to his side. Kat had her fist pressed against her tightly closed lips. She watched the stage with grim determination, but her cheeks were wet with tears. Surreptitiously, he pulled out his handkerchief and passed it to her.

As if sensing the crowd was reaching its emotional limits, the song changed again. The tempo remained contemplative, but the key changed, reassuring with notes and tones that spoke of healing and hope. Then it grew past comfort to determination before ending with one last, optimistic, victorious note.

Marisol lowered her instrument and regarded the audience, panting and elated.

For a long moment, there was silence. Then LeRoy leaped to his feet with a howl of approval. Everyone stood, and the room echoed with applause.

Laughing, her own eyes misty with tears, Marisol bowed, then gestured to her father. He shook his head and directed the adulation back to her.

After that performance, the finale was anticlimactic, but no variety show is complete without everyone doing the last song-and-dance and taking another bow. Then, Gloria Joy stepped forward for her farewell speech.

"...We leave you now to continue your adventures among the stars. But in the universe of our lives, love is many stars. The warm glow of a parent for a child. The bright shine of new love or the steadfast glow of longtime friendship. Even the erratic twinkle of a sister's love for her bratty brother!" She glanced backstage and giggled. "Space is vast and empty. And yet, we don't see that. We see the stars. As you look at your own lives—past, present, and future—it's my wish-upon-a-star that you see the starlight that comes from love."

***

The next day...

The reception area for the airlock was filled with people saying, "Goodbye."

Gel was getting some last-minute ribbing from his old coworkers about his new officer status. He didn't mind. He was too proud. Besides, he didn't have ribs—but he did have a bright future.

Leslie was making her farewells to more than a few new friends. Later that evening, there would be a couple of barfights as those who thought they had an exclusive learned the hard way that Leslie was glad to share.

Gloria Joy tried to tickle her brother into giggling. Dolfrick stoically refused, but he did give her a big hug.

Ellie and Todd kissed and kissed and in between kisses, talked over each other.

"So you find out your mom's delivery schedule—"

-kiss-

"There has to be a time when your parents can get away."

-kiss-

"They'll drop everything. I'll make them. I have an in with DipCorps after the KeepOut incident."

-kiss-

"I love you!"

"I love you more!"

"I love you, forever!"

"I love you many stars..."

A few paces away, Jeb, Phineas, and Katika watched with bemused expressions.

"How long have they been together?" Kat asked.

"Five days," Jeb answered. He'd never admit it, but he thought they were cuter than prairie dogs rubbing noses.

Katika rolled her eyes. Then she opened her arms to hug Phineas. "It's been so good to see you again," she told him.

"It's been good to see you at all. Don't scare us like that again."

"No promises."

She turned to Jeb. "We'll be done with repairs in a couple of weeks. Think you can keep out of trouble until then?"

"No promises."

They lingered there, smiling at each other, enjoying the growing tension of attraction, knowing one of them would break it.

Well, knowing she'd break it. Jeb was too much of a gentleman. Ladies, first, and all that.

Finally, she grabbed his shirt and pulled him down until his lips met hers.

He wrapped his arms around her and bent her into a dip for a kiss worthy of two accomplished captains.

When at last, he stood her upright, she was blushing and breathless.

"Be good, Texas." She poked his chest playfully, then strode away.

"I'm always good!" he protested to her retreating back.

Then, he winked at his first officer and best friend. "Sometimes, I'm even better."

As they started back to their ship, Phin asked, with mock longsuffering, "Will this last you?"

"Yeah," Jeb drawled. "Leastways, until I see her again."

Captain's Log, Intergalactic Date 676959.34

All systems are running green, and that applies to my crew as well as my ship. It's a nice feeling. We didn't get to spend as much time on station as I'd like, but the time we had was well spent. We got a lot done and managed to make some fond memories and new relationships to carry us on our next big adventure.

Captains' Cage Match

Captain's Log, Intergalactic Date 676999.55

We continue to be in hot pursuit of the unknown aliens that massacred our outpost on Festus Three.

Captain Jebediah Tiberius leaned forward and glared at the viewscreen as if he could will his ship to move faster. They were already at Warp 10 with the engines redlined and Commander Deary wailing and cussing, yet they were gaining at a snail's pace. At least they were gaining. They just had to overtake the bloodthirsty sonnobiches before they reached home—or reinforcements.

That was the problem with space pursuits. They were either done quick or went on for hours, even days. Deary had made it clear that the Impulsive could not keep this speed for days, and they were too far from Union Space to get reinforcements themselves.

In fact, they'd been heading back to the nearest starbase to drop off Lieutenant Ellie Doall so she could make the long trip back to Sapphire to meet her fiancé's family when they got a call from Festus Three inviting them to a layover. Jeb had declined, but when a more insistent invitation came, Ellie noticed something odd about the transmission, and they'd gone in under Yellow Alert to investigate. That caution had saved them from getting ambushed with crewmen on the planet. They'd engaged the enemy, who ran.

And, four hours later, they were still running. He'd brought the ship back to Yellow Alert after the first hour, but fury kept him wound up as if they were in battle.

Jeb was typing in a note to put Lieutenant Doall in for a commendation when she said, "Captain, there's a solar system coming up to starboard. I'm picking up transmissions. They're scanning us."

"I see it," Lieutenant Tonio Cruz, the pilot replied. "The other ship is skirting it. Not like purposely avoiding it, just racing past."

"Can you gain any ground if we warp through it?" Jeb asked. "Lieutenant Doall, how dangerous are those signals? Can you hail them?"

Before either lieutenant could answer, Ellie called, "Sir! The other ship is slowing. Warp Six...Warp Four...One... Sublight... Sir, they are at a dead stop."

Commander Phineas Smythe, First Officer, furrowed his brow. "Did they burn out their engines?"

Jeb frowned. "That, or they've decided to fight. At least we're away from that solar system. All hands, Red Alert. Wikadas shields on full, weapons ready—"

His next commands were interrupted as everyone was thrown forward. As readers of Space Traipse know, the Impulsive is equipped with interior shakers to jerk the ship when something strikes the shields. It helps the crew maintain a sense of urgency and feel like the ship is being hurt, rather than having light beams bouncing off the deflector shields.

This was not what was happening.

"Capitano!" Cruz cried, "We're losing speed! Warp Five...Two. We've stopped!" His hands flew over his controls, pressing buttons that seemed totally random to the casual observer, but were in fact only partially random as his frustration increased. Finally, he smacked the console. "It's no good sir! The engines won't respond."

At the weapons console, Lieutenant Enigo Guiermo Ricardo Montoya Guiterrez LaFuentes was doing something similar. "Weapons are dead, too, Captain. Shields are still up."

"Bridge to Engineering," Jeb called.

The voice of Commander Deary replied, "Don't even ask, sair. Everything's working, but nothing is getting to propulsion or weapons. I dinnae know why, but we're working on it. In the meantime, life support and all other systems are operational."

"Do what you can, Angus." Jeb turned to look at Ops. "Scanners? Did we run into some kind of cosmic tar pit or something?"

They'd seen stranger.

But Lieutenant Doall shook her head. "Scanners only report normal space. The alien ship is similarly stuck… Sir, I think something from that solar system is doing it."

"What? This far out? Is it a tractor beam?"

"Not that we'd recognize. Ensign Gel O'Tin wins the WTF pool."

Despite the tense situation they were in, several crewmen groaned enviously. Since the janbots had all been destroyed, winnings were in chore vouchers. Gel would be living easy for weeks.

"Incoming transmission," Ellie said, though she didn't really need to. At that moment, all the lights flickered, and then the viewscreen came alive with psychedelic colors as if the Impulsive had just tripped acid and was listening to Pink Floyd. If "Dark Side of the Moon" started playing, Jeb would have to order a complete shutdown and reset.

Fortunately, a haughty male voice came on. "We are the Arragantons. You and the other ship have intruded in our space on a mission of violence. This is not permissible. Our analysis of your library files shows your violent tendencies are inherent. So be it. We will control them. We will resolve your conflict in the way most suited to your limited mentalities."

"Signs," Jeb muttered. "Why doesn't anybody put up signs?"

"It didn't work for KeepOut," Commander Smythe shrugged.

The voice of the Arraganton ignored them. "Captain Jebediah Tiberius. We have prepared a planet with a suitable atmosphere. There you and the captain of the Sllth ship you are pursuing will settle your dispute. We will provide each of you a recording-translating device. Use it so that a chronicle of this contest will serve to dissuade others of your kind from entering our system."

"A navigational buoy would be more effective!"

"You will not be permitted to communicate with your ship. You will each be totally alone."

"Now, just hold on a minute!"

"We have supplied sufficient elements for either of you to construct weapons lethal enough to destroy the other, which seems to be your intention. The contest will be one of ingenuity against ingenuity, brute strength against brute strength. We will allow the winner to go his way unharmed. We will destroy the loser, along with his ship, in the interests of peace. The results will be final."

"How is that peaceful?" Jeb demanded, fully aware of the irony of his statement, considering blasting the aliens to smithereens was his intention in the first place. Meanwhile, Lt. LaFuentes was saying, "Take me!"

"There will be no discussion. It is done."

And Jeb was whisked off the bridge.

* * *

Captain's Log, Intergalactic Date 676999.67

The Impulsive is stuck in space like a mallard in an oil slick, and somehow, I have been yanked off the bridge and deposited on some unknown planet with the captain of the alien ship. Weaponless and trapped, I'm stuck in a cage match against the creature the Arragantons called a Sllth, and damn if he ain't big, ugly, and stupid-looking—kind of like some ancient costume of a reptilian life form. I gotta remember that he's an intelligent, highly advanced individual, the captain of a starship, like me, and like me, a dangerously clever opponent.

He tried to hit me with a stick. I threw a rock at him.

It didn't take Jeb more than a couple of minutes to learn that hand-to-hand combat against the Sllth was a great way to get himself—and the Impulsive—stupidly killed. So, he chose the better part of valor and ran like crazy, pausing only long enough to throw the biggest stone he could. Naturally, it bounced off the Sllth as if it were Styrofoam, and the alien captain then picked up a rock five times bigger and nearly hit Jeb.

Ten minutes and two miles later, Jeb had reached the following conclusions:

- The Sllth was big, ugly, stupid-looking, and strong!
- He was also a lot slower than Jeb.
- While the planet had a lot of interesting minerals, there wasn't much in terms of ready weapons, especially ones that would take out a foe at a distance. He'd have to get creative.
- Jeb needed more cardio in his workouts.

As Jeb walked out a cramp in his side, he ascended a convenient hill that stood higher than the rest and looked around. No sign of the Sllth anywhere. Time to stop and think.

The Arragantons said they'd provided everything needed to construct weapons, but they also said it was a battle of wits as well as strength. So they must have intended more than hurling rocks at each other.

Maybe I can outlast him, the lazy part of Jeb's mind considered. How long could a Sllth go without food or water?

Jeb sighed. The Geckans, also reptilian-based, had been known to survive a week. Plus, if he delayed this, when he got back, he'd probably have to face another cage match against a lovelorn lieutenant who'd been denied the chance to see her fiancé. Besides, who knew if there was food here either of them could eat, much less water.

What had he seen in his "strategic retreat"? Rocks, scrub brush, salt deposits, brittlebush, juniper trees, some of which had been burned in a fire.... A lot like where he grew up, but no cactus, which would have been useful, and no rattlers, which was a relief. But then, there was stuff that didn't belong in the climate: a bamboo-like plant, a sulfur deposit, vines that were thick as ropes.

There were caves, too: shallow things carved into the cliffs, lots of rocks on the hills above.

Why was everything coming back to rocks?

And, of course, there was this recorder/translator device so he could "record the proceedings for posterity." You'd think with a species advanced enough to stop his ship and teleport him who-knew-where, they could just record the proceedings themselves.

Maybe they were.

The device was simple enough. It looked like the hilt of a light saber and had only an on/off button. He clicked it on. "This is Captain Tiberius calling the Arragantons. Y'all there watching us? I hope you're bored."

When there was no reply, he tried again. "Captain Tiberius to the Sllth captain. Please respond."

He waited, glared at the device, turned it off and turned it back on. "This is Captain Jebediah Tiberius of the HuFleet Ship Impulsive, recording in hopes that it gets back to HuFleet and Union Command. I'm engaged in personal combat with a creature apparently called a Sllth. Huge bugger, plus ugly and stupid-looking—"

"Is this how you expect to win, human? With insults?"

Gotcha! "Well, how-do? Now that we can understand each other, how about we talk this out? Right now, I'd rather we both get off this planet."

"Why would I cooperate with invaders?"

"Invaders? Festus Three? It was uninhabited."

"It is in Sllth territory."

"Well, how were we supposed to know that? There weren't no signs, no space markers. Humans are squatters—most sapient species are. We see a nice planet, we check for sentient life. If we don't find any, we set up housekeeping."

"You invaded Sllth lands. We acted in our empire's defense."

"I don't like your attitude! First off, you didn't say anything, not in the thirteen years that colony had been there. Then you went in, guns blazing, and killed them all. Spouses, children... Innocents!"

"None are innocent."

Jeb clicked off the switch to give himself time to glare at the sky and heave a big sigh. Then he tried again, "Look. How about we let your empire leaders hash this out with my Union's leaders?"

"Now who is stupid?"

"We both are if we keep on with this cage match for the Arragantons' amusement. How about we combine forces and go kick their butts instead?"

"And then what? You will take their planet as you sought to take ours?"

The Sllth said more, but it was mostly insults, some untranslatable, but all convincing Jeb that negotiating was not going to work.

"You know? I'm kind of leaning back to big, ugly, and stupid. Why don't you come find me?"

He switched off the device.

"All righty, then!" he said to the world in general. "Let's do this."

He started down the hill to where he'd seen a cave that might work for his purposes. Along the way, he paused when something glinty caught his eye. "Diamonds? More rocks?"

Still, they were one of the hardest substances known. He pulled off his shirt, tied knots high in the sleeves, filled both with diamonds of varying sizes, then tied knots in the cuffs.

Two hours later, Jeb had made himself a nice "camp" among a clump of Cyprus and surrounded it with traps. That was his fallback if his main idea didn't work. He used a branch of a bush to clear away any of his tracks as he left the spot.

Then he went to work on a cliffside he'd seen, with a cave below a precariously balanced pile of rocks. Using vines and pitons made from tree branches, he set up trip lines, and a rope he could pull to bring down the rocks. Best case, he'd crush the Sllth captain; if not, he might trap him. Maybe that would satisfy the Arragantons.

Now to draw the Sllth to the trap. The sun had passed its zenith and the temperature was dropping. A cozy fire sounded like the perfect lure, especially since he'd found some flint. He gathered the sticks and kindling into a wide piece of bamboo he'd scavenged and entered the cave.

Once there, though, he stopped and gaped at the fine, white substance on the ground. Was that saltpeter? Jeb laughed. *Sllth, you're so screwed!*

He dumped everything out of the bamboo and started shoveling the potassium nitrate into it with his bare hands.

He almost didn't hear the Sllth enter the cave until it was too late.

Fortunately, the alien's breath was loud, and he was able to leap to his feet before it let out an unintelligible roar. The trip lines also slowed the Sllth as he maneuvered over them. He swung wide-armed at Jeb, who managed to duck under and shoot past, cradling his find against his chest.

Jeb ran, stepping lightly between the trip lines...until the Sllth hooked his shirt in his claw. The shirt, designed to be sturdy and nearly indestructible except when certain plot devices...er, stresses were applied to it, tore. He was free, but it messed with his balance.

His foot caught on the last trip line.

He kept running as rocks pelted him from above. One barked his ankle enough to make him howl, but he didn't stop until he was well away from the rockfall and his foe. Panting with fright and pain, he turned around.

The cave was now closed off by a pile of rocks, the Sllth inside. Jeb started to cheer, but then the rocks began to shift.

Jeb swore and limped away. At least he had another plan, but he had materials to gather first.

* * *

Jeb's great grandfather, Jebediah Cornelius Tiberius, had had a brief and unsatisfactory enlistment in Union fleet before returning home to the family ranch. His son, Jebediah Zane Tiberius, had followed in the ranching tradition, developing a strong interest in the cottage industries of historical crafting and petroleum refining. Jeb's father had joined HuFleet, so many of Jeb's formative years were spent with his grandfather, learning to do things like convert crude oil into cold cream, ride horses, and make gunpowder.

While the Sllth dug itself slowly from the rubble, Jeb gathered the needed ingredients. There was no way to measure them exactly, but using a cup-like piece of the translator device's casing, he was able to get a good approximation of the proportions. (He chuckled, remembering the time when he thought he could measure them by hand and nearly blew up the barn. He was...eleven? Yeah, Grandma had sworn he'd never live to see twelve.)

The Sllth had almost cleared a hole big enough to crawl through. Jeb gulped and amended his description to include "freakishly strong."

Next, the diamonds. Then bury one end into the ground. After all, this was a pipe bomb more than a mortar and he wanted to see his next birthday.

The Sllth was out. He stood, slightly bloodied, trailing the vines used to spill the rocks. He bore discolorations on his skin indicating bruises, but still very hale—and very angry.

Thread in the fuse. Strike the flame.

The spark fizzled.

The Sllth advanced, still slow, but way too fast for Jeb's liking. Strike the flame...

The Sllth roared, and Jeb didn't need a translation device to know the alien's murderous intent.

Come on, flame! In desperation, he tried to light it closer to the mortar. This time, it took, but before he could back away, the bomb went off, destroying the bamboo and smacking him hard against a cliff. The world grayed around him, but he fought to stay conscious. Through blurred vision, he saw the Sllth jerk back, its chest pocked with diamonds and bloody. Then, it toppled.

Jeb forced himself to his feet and groggily made his way to the alien captain. He was still breathing.

"You gotta be kidding me." Adding, "too ornery to die" to his list, he grabbed the ropes and put to use another skill he'd learned on the ranch. In 11 seconds, he had the Sllth's wrists and ankles tied together. Gramps would grumble at how slow he was, but the world kept tilting.

Jeb stood, ignoring the way the ground listed, and threw his arms in the air, rodeo style. "All right, Arragantons. That's it! In the tradition of my people, I have won!"

The Sllth disappeared, and on the top of the hill stood a young humanish man with blond hair and a flowing white robe. He had a shiny aura, too, though that could have been Jeb's eyes playing tricks.

Jeb squinted. "You're an Arraganton?"

The being smiled benevolently. "Does my appearance surprise you, Captain?"

"I was expecting someone a little more..."

Before he could finish his sentence, the Arraganton jumped to his own conclusions. "I am nearly twelve hundred Union years old. You surprise me, Captain."

"Just you?"

"You spared a helpless enemy while believing that, if the tables were turned, he'd have killed you. That's the advanced trait of mercy."

"Ya don't say?" Jeb's head was starting to pound. He wouldn't mind a little mercy, himself, in the form of a hypospray of imposazine.

"We did not expect this. We feel there may be hope for your kind. Therefore, we will not destroy you or your ship. It would not be civilized."

"As opposed to kidnapping two sapient beings and forcing them to fight to the death? I'm not sure that word means what you think it means. What'd you do with the Sllth?"

"We've returned him to his ship. If you like, I shall destroy him for you."

"Oh, yeah. That's 'civilized.' I think your translator needs adjusting. Anyway. Don't. If they thought we were invaders, then there might be a way to salvage this without more killing."

The Arraganton beamed at Jeb as if he were a precocious child. "Very good, Captain! There is hope for you. You are still half savage, but perhaps—in a few millennia—we shall reach out to your people."

Jeb was just biting back a sarcastic reply when he suddenly found himself on the bridge of the Impulsive.

"Captain!" people cheered, then exclaimed in concern and surprise when they took in his bruises and the bloody scrapes on his exposed back where he'd smacked the cliff and rocks and sticks had gotten through his torn shirt. The noise felt like gongs banging in his ears. Things were getting blurry and tilty again, and he seriously did not want to throw up in front of his crew.

Commander Smythe said, "Jeb, are you all right?"

"Nope," was all he could manage before he passed out.

Acting Captain's Log, Intergalactic Date 676999.93, Commander Phineas Smythe reporting

I've taken over the captain's duties while Captain Tiberius is in Sickbay recovering from a severe concussion caused by the homemade pipe bomb he used to defeat the Sllth. The Arragantons had "graciously" broadcasted the last few minutes of the battle, starting with just after the cave-in and ending with the captain's rodeo-style victory. Please see attached.

After returning him to the ship, the Arragantons transported us into Union Space, which they could find thanks to the territorial marker buoys we set up. It's unclear what happened to the Sllth, although we assume the Arragantons kept their promise and returned them to their own space.

We are heading back to Festus Three to assess damage, seek survivors, and retrieve or destroy any surviving technology before abandoning the colony. It will be up to the diplomats to make a determination on who has rights.

The Arragantons said we "held promise for a half-savage race." I can't help but wonder if they understand just how many races there are in the galaxy, and how widely ranging they are in philosophies, attitudes, and simple violent instinct. They have said it may take several thousand years before we are ready to meet them, but it could be that they will need that long before they are ready to meet us.

Naked Impulse

Acting Captain's Log, Intergalactic Date 677001.32, Commander Phineas Smythe reporting

Captain Tiberius is recovering nicely from his concussion after single-handedly fighting the Sllth, a buff, lizard-like alien against whom he was pitted to prove which species was most worthy of getting away with kicking the other's arse. Doc Sorcha has allowed him to return to his quarters to rest but will not allow him back on duty until he remembers how he tore his shirt.

In the meantime, the Union has noted the Arraganton's conclusion that we "might be worthy of their friendship in a thousand years" and had flagged the species as DNE-GOT (Do Not Engage Until They Get Over Themselves).

We're about to investigate the HMB Marvin, which failed to make its regular check-ins twice. Although on the edge of Cyber territory, the Cybers have been completely silent since the incident at Filedise, so we're expecting it's just a mechanical error. But if not, we're hoping that we will find some clue to lead us to our missing comrades.

We found the ship orbiting a red supergiant that is collapsing into a white dwarf. This was not where it should have been, and the only explanation for the change in mission was in the captain's last transmission: "Watching it being disintegrated makes me angry. Very angry indeed."

We've found several airlocks open, and all systems shut down, but no other external signs of violence. Commander Deary and his team went first and have restored basic power and environmental controls. I'm leaving Commander Paolinelli in charge while I join the team to investigate the ship.

The HMB Marvin lacked a second bridge control, so everyone teleported to the engineering section. The air was cold enough to cause fog to come out of their mouths when they spoke, and even the special weave of their uniforms did not stop some people from shivering. However, the ghastly scene before them was as much to blame.

The engineering section was littered with dead and frozen bodies, but not the kind of corpses you'd find if a hatch had been blown or there'd been a malfunction that the crew had died trying to fix. Several bodies lay broken and tangled near the warp core; another slumped in front of an outlet. Two pairs of legs stuck out of a Jeffries tube. It wasn't clear how they died, but there was no doubt what they'd been doing.

Toward the environmental section, another corpse slumped in her seat, as if she'd fallen asleep at her post after turning off the environmental controls. Doc Sorcha was examining the body. She alone of the Impulsive away team did not wear protective gloves. As a photonic being, she was not in danger of contracting any biological agents.

Trash littered the room, and not the kind of debris expected after a fight or a desperate attempt to save a ship. Rather, they saw bottles and sweets, toys, and abandoned articles of clothing.

Lieutenant Leslie Straus stepped up to one corpse and pulled something from his hair. She rubbed it between her gloved fingers, then wiped it off on the dead person's uniform sleeve. She looked at her hands and did it again. She tsked with disgust when the shiny bits still didn't all come off.

"Glitter?" she asked.

"Aye!" Commander Deary exclaimed. He sounded especially affronted, and with good reason. Any hint of the pernicious substance on an on-duty engineering crewman was grounds for court-martial. Yet, he had counted at least six people who sparkled.

Enigo was on the second-level section which opened to the warp core. "Commander Smythe," he called out, "from here, it looks like those people jumped."

"Suicides?" Smythe asked. That didn't match the profile of the average HuFleet spaceman, much less a handful all at once and on the same ship.

LaFuentes pointed to one. "I dunno. If they'd wanted to off themselves, they could have jumped straight into the warp core. Instead, they all have partial burns. Look how that one's hands are reaching out. It was like he was trying to jump the gap and brushed against the shields."

"So, this was a game?" Lieutenant Ellie Doall, the operations officer, asked. Smythe had brought her on the away mission because he'd hoped the challenge would keep her mind off the fact that she'd not been able to visit her fiancé as planned. Now, he wondered if she might not have been happier sulking on the Impulsive's bridge. He was rather thinking he would. The whole scene was reminding him of one of the creepier episodes of his favorite show.

Smythe turned to Deary, "What do the engineering logs say?"

In response, Deary waved a hand at the charred corpse. "There arnae any. This walloper here made sure of that. We checked the environmental controls, however, and we didn't see any indications of an airborne agent."

Doc Sorcha left the body she was examining to join them. "I've not found any traces of viruses or bacteria, Commander. It looks like a bizarre case of mass hypoxia. There have been previously recorded incidents of similarly odd behavior, usually on smaller ships. The 'space loonies,' it's called. However, I've only examined one body thoroughly, which is not enough to make a conclusion. I'd like to go to Sickbay and see if there are any medical logs, or better yet, patients I can thaw in quarantine and examine. In the meantime, I advise everyone to keep their gloves on and do not touch the bodies unless necessary. We should also do a full decontamination."

"Is the bridge safe?" Smythe asked the chief engineer.

Deary nodded. "We've got a forcefield in place and it's holding atmosphere, but I wouldnae trust it for long. Some radge blasted a hole through their dome. Why they put the bridge on the top of a ship is beyond me. Stupidly vulnerable, it is."

Smythe nodded. "I couldn't agree more. There should be copies of the logs in auxiliary control. Lieutenant LaFuentes, you and Ensign Becca escort the doctor to Sickbay. Straus, Doall, and I shall make our way to the bridge. The rest of you work with Commander Deary. Commander, can we make the ship tow-worthy?"

"Aye. We'll check the status of the structural integrity fields, but it shouldnae take much."

"Once you're done, return to the ship and undergo decontamination and full examination. That goes for everyone. Let's not take chances."

* * *

Ellie felt a tad bit guilty about feeling glad to be on the away team. True, they were walking around a virtual graveyard, but at least everyone seemed to have died happy. She glanced at the couple in the Jeffries tube. Some died very happy, indeed.

She missed Todd.

She blamed her parents. They kept pushing off deciding on a date to meet at the starbase until she'd finally given up and resolved to go to Sapphire station on Europa and visit Todd's family alone. By the time she had the travel arrangements figured out, the Impulsive ended up pursuing the Sllthan ship, and her plans toppled like dominoes. Now, each lead on the Cybers was taking them farther from him.

We knew this would happen, she told herself. She had another two to five years on the Impulsive, and there was nothing for a civilian on this ship. She could probably request a transfer, but this was where she wanted to be. She wasn't ready to give it up, not even for him. But, oh, she missed him.

She acknowledged the doctor's recommendations and Commander Smythe's orders, then followed Leslie out of Engineering. They'd take the lazivator up to the bridge. The air was starting to warm up, but before they left, she suggested they keep the temperature at freezing.

"Good idea," Enigo agreed as he slid down the ladder. "That way, we don't have to worry about slipping on blood."

He stepped over a body of a crewman that had impaled himself on a broken bar.

"A sensible precaution. Make it so," Smythe said because although the accepted HuFleet term was "Beer me," as a member of British nobility, he could never make those words sound natural in a command situation.

So, each party headed off on their tasks, all chilly except for the doctor. Doc Sorcha debated altering her program to manifest goosebumps in a show of sympathy, then decided everyone was too focused on the tragedy around them for it to matter.

One problem with the cold, however, was that it made it harder to detect bodies accurately. The Marvin housed 101 crewmen. They'd found 10 partying it up in Engineering, and two actually at their posts, though what they'd been doing was anyone's guess. One presumably turned off the environmental systems but may have been trying to fix them. The other had been rewiring the weapons systems into something he had called the "Illudium Pew-36," according to the schematics.

They found seven more outside, orbiting the ship like gruesome human satellites, and two others that had been caught in the pull of the star. That left 80 more to account for. The odds of surviving were less than a percent, but they needed to account for everyone to be sure.

They found another body clawing at the lazivator doors.

"That's more than a little spooky," Lieutenant Straus said, and with the commander's permission, carefully moved it from the doorway.

The door nonetheless refused to open as their warm bodies approached. Leslie opened the console to hotwire the control. While they waited, Ellie contemplated the body. 79, then. Why was he trying to get to the lazivator? Was he trying to escape? Flee? Hide?

Hide!

"Commander," Ellie said, "we should send someone to check the shuttles to make sure no one was hiding there. Someone might be alive but so close to death, we're not picking them up through the extra barriers. We might want to check the teleporter buffers as well."

"Excellent suggestions," Smythe said and called the Impulsive to send landing parties to those sections.

"Got it!" Leslie declared as the doors swung open.

Ellie had just enough time to scream and try to leap out of the way as dozens of frozen bodies spilled out of the lift and half-buried her and Commander Smythe.

"Ellie! Commander!" Leslie called out as an avalanche of bodies fell on her friend and their first officer. Without thinking, she dug into the pile of bodies, caught Ellie by the arm, and pulled her out. She moved to go after the commander, but he'd already managed to dig himself clear.

"Bloody hell!" he shouted, his eyes wider than she'd ever seen. He stared at the pile of corpses like he expected them to rise up and chase him. He didn't look injured, but he did have frost on his hair and face from the bodies.

Ellie managed to stop shrieking, but her hands trembled as she examined her scanning equipment. "Sir, there are 43 bodies here. Different ranks, different departments... I don't think they are all from this level."

Commander Smythe rubbed his hair. Flakes of frost came off. "So much for not touching any of the bodies. Smythe to Doc Sorcha. It seems we've had skin-to-skin contact with multiple corpses." He shivered, then relayed the details.

"We are almost to Sickbay. We'll know more if this is a problem after I've scanned the logs and looked around. Why don't you complete your tasks on the bridge, then meet me there?"

Enigo cut in, "Did you say forty-three? The Marvin has Type II lazivators. Safety regs allow for a maximum of 15 in emergencies."

"And has anything you've seen today indicated the crew was safety-conscious?" Commander Smythe asked dryly.

"No, sir. My point, though, is that it's a challenge to see how many people you can cram in. Union record is 42. Straus, look to see if anyone was trying to squeeze in from the top."

"Yes, sir." Biting a grimace, she edged around the blocked-open entrance, stepping as carefully over the bodies as she could. She stuck only her torso in as she looked around. "Good thinking, sir. I see two more."

Ellie gulped. Thirty-six left to account for.

Commander Smythe let out a sigh. "Let's log their identities, then. They may as well get recognition for their efforts, ill-fated as they were. However, all things considered, I think I'd prefer to take the stairs."

* * *

Ensign Daphne Becca waited until the security chief had signed off before asking, "Did you ever try to break the lazivator crowd record, sir?"

"Nah, but I've had to break up an unauthorized attempt or three. At the very least, people should try it when the lazivator is sitting at the lowest level. That's only common sense, but some people..."

Truth to tell, she didn't really care. She was just making conversation to take her mind off the mission. Ever since the cybervirus had played pranks with the artificial gravity and caused her to topple onto the captain multiple times, revealing her secret crush, she'd been wary of away missions. Usually, when an underling developed romantic feelings for a bridge officer, they were put on missions where they either fell in love with an alien or died a horrible but heroic death. Unless they found some hot dude in a stasis chamber, she was going to have to tread very carefully.

I could get a job in the private sector, she thought. I'm a pilot, not a....whatever it is they think qualifies me to be on this cockamamie mission.

They were coming upon Sickbay. To the right and left were doors to the labs. As she passed by one, it opened, and a body toppled out. She shrieked and blundered into Lieutenant LaFuentes.

He grabbed her by the arms before she fell over. "Easy, Ensign Becca. You're safe. You can't be much safer than with the Chief of Security, right?"

"And if you should be injured," Doc Sorcha said as she opened the doors to Sickbay, "the Chief Medical Officer is only two paces away. How much safer can you get?"

The doctor crossed the threshold, and an anvil fell on her head.

Ensign Becca screamed again and started to run, but Enigo held her fast. "Don't move!" When she had calmed, he tapped his communicator.

"LaFuentes to away teams. The ship is booby-trapped. I repeat, there are lethal traps set on the ship. Watch for tripwires, pause before going through doors. We've lost the doctor. She's been crushed by a large, heavy..."

"Anvil," Becca finished for him. "It's used in blacksmithing. We had them in the colony where I grew up."

As she continued to babble something about horseshoes and kitchen hooks, he finished his report to the first officer.

Commander Deary's voice came next, "Lieutenant, what kind of damage did the doctor sustain?"

Enigo replied, "We don't see her at all. The weight must have been more than her matrix could handle. Ensign Becca and I are going to see if we can remove the anvil. Standby."

Scanners out and moving slowly, they entered Sickbay. Whoever set the trap made no attempt to hide the mechanism, which was set to deploy when the doors opened. To the side were two more crewmen, one in a lab coat, curled up on the floor, clutching their stomachs, mouths open as if in pain.

Or laughter? That was sick, if so. Even on the Hood, they wouldn't have thought that kind of death funny.

The anvil was pulled up by ropes and pulleys. LaFuentes grabbed the crank and pulled, muscles straining, but the device, which had fallen so easily, resisted his efforts to raise it. After several minutes of grunting and sweating, he managed to get it a couple of feet off the ground.

He swore. This was too much effort. Time to think like a security officer. "Ensign, shoot it."

"What?"

He grunted as the heavy object fought to fall back on the ground. "Pull out your raser, set it to disintegrate, and shoot the anvil!"

"Oh!" She did as instructed, but instead of glowing yellow, then white, then disappearing in a glittery display, it blasted apart with a poof of glowing hot dust-size particles.

Both Becca and he were blown back. She landed between the bodies and scrambled away. He struck a wall with a painful thump that knocked the air out of him. He slid to the floor and stayed there a minute until the dizziness passed. They were both covered in fine dust.

"Lieutenant!" Becca grabbed a couple of towels from a drawer and ran to him. "Are you all right? I'm sorry. I don't know what happened."

"Not your fault. Someone designed it that way. Who knows why." With a small groan, he pulled himself up and went to check the remains of the holographic doctor. As he'd guessed, her body was not there; rather, a crushed box that was her holoemitter testified to her untimely demise.

Acting Captain's Log, Supplemental

The loss of the holoemitter for our emergency medical photonic technician has made this mission even grimmer, but at least no one else was hurt and her original program is "alive" and well in our Sickbay, and the two had been exchanging data continuously. Commander Deary is taking the remains of the portable emitter back to the Impulsive to try to repair it.

Commander Angus Deary didn't want to admit it, but he might have made a mistake patterning the holographic doctor after his old girlfriend, Simone. He was taking the destruction of the portable holographic generator more personally than he should.

Ah, but she was the most beautiful woman he'd ever seen, with her fine skin and mysterious eyes and the way she used to smile at him...

What happened to us? he wondered as he blew dust off one of the pieces of the broken components.

"Here." The ensign who had accompanied LaFuentes and the doctor handed him a sealable bag to put the components in. She and LaFuentes were also coated in the fine dust. He snatched it from her hands and gently settled the pieces into it, wincing as they clacked against each other.

Enigo returned from his patrol of Sickbay. "The area is clear," he said.

Deary snarled, "Oh, aye! Ye check now, do ye? What about before Doc Sorcha walked into a trap?"

"Ay! How was I supposed to know?" the chief of security snapped back.

"Isnae that your job?" Deary shoved the last piece into the bag, sealed it with an angry swipe, and stood to glare down at Enigo's frowning face.

Deary towered over Enigo, but that didn't stop the angry Hoodian from stepping closer and glaring back at his superior officer. He yelled, "How was I supposed to prepare for some crazed medical officer deciding to smash his patients with a rock?"

"Anvil," Ensign Becca said.

Both men snapped, "Whatever!" and she shrank back.

Enigo clenched his fists tightly, then forced himself to take a deep breath and calm down. "Listen, sir, contrary to popular belief, I cannot anticipate everything. I cannot see into the future. If I could, Loreli would be…"

He pressed his lips tightly together, looked away, and tried again. "Everyone has been warned. We're being more careful. Let's just be glad that it was the holodoc that got damaged and not a real person killed."

"I'm a real person," the ensign murmured.

Deary turned to her. "Do ye not have work to do, Missy?"

She gaped at him. "I'm a qualified pilot. I fly ships. What do I know about medicine?"

Enigo sneered, "Do qualified pilots know how to download mission logs?"

"Oh, right. Yes, sir."

When she skulked off, Deary turned back to Enigo. "And you. Your job is to protect all the members of our crew, not just the biological ones. I never want to hear you say that Simone isn't a real person."

"Who?"

"Ach, never mind!" He slapped his comm badge. "Deary to Teleporter Room Three. Beam me directly to Sickbay, and Dour—do nae forget the decontamination sequence."

The teleporter chief must have picked up on his mood because he didn't make his usual annoyingly prophetic statements but did as he was told.

The air of the Impulsive hit him like an oven blast after the chill on the Marvin, which only annoyed him more. But then, *she* appeared before him and everything felt better.

"Simone."

The vision of Simone frowned and said, "Commander, you are not well." He knew then this was the holodoc, the bastardization of the woman he'd loved, programmed to give the EMPT a more pleasing appearance and mannerisms. It had never loved him. It couldn't help him now.

But he could change that.

"Computer, Engineering override, Deary 36-SIM-24-ON-38-E. Freeze the EMPT program."

"Wait!" the doc said, then froze, mouth partly open and one foot stepping forward.

He looked her over. She was so beautiful, so close to the real thing. It wouldn't take much to complete the conversion. He set the bag with the portable emitter on a counter, then went to the programming console and got to work.

"Ah, lassie, I've waited long enough," he told the static image of his former love.

* * *

Acting Captain's Log, Intergalactic Date 677001.33

We've completed our mission of downloading logs and accounting for all the crewmen. As Lieutenant Doall suspected, we did find a couple in the back seats of a shuttle, but they were obviously not hiding. We also found 17 in the mess hall. One wall had been painted with the words, "Halt and be fricasseed." Six of the crewmen were near the wall, apparently dodging shots from another crewman. It seemed to be a game. There was even a table set up for taking bets. The rest of the crew were in various parts of the ship, but few at their duty stations.

The remainder we found in their quarters, having died in their sleep.

The ship is in towable condition, so we should be able to bring it back with us. I've instructed the engineering team to turn the environmental controls off again, however. Despite the computer's insistence that the temperature is set to just below freezing, I don't want to chance the bodies putrefying en route.

The decontamination sequence on a teleporter is a marvel, as it can remove any particulates on the body down to a molecular level, and it knows what constitutes a "body." It removed the slight sheen of sweat starting to form on Phineas' brow and all the dust from Enigo and Becca but did not remove so much as a hair from their arms, for example. However, what it could not do was remove anything that was already entangled in the body itself.

Rather, it could, when used by a very capable teleporter chief and usually at great cost to the system and some danger to the participant, and then only in very particular plot needs...er, physical conditions.

All this is to explain how the away teams could go through decontamination and still experience the events we all know are coming.

Commander Phineas Smythe stepped off the teleporter dais, his brow furrowed with confusion. "Chief, I thought you were sending us directly to Sickbay."

Dour replied with his usual tone, which is to say, he made the next words sound like a proclamation of doom. "The doctor contacted me as I was initiating teleport. She said she wishes to examine each of you individually and will contact you once she has finished with Commander Deary. Until then, she wants all of you to self-quarantine in your quarters."

"Fine by me," Lt. LaFuentes muttered. He plopped his tricorder into Lt. Straus's hands and stormed out without waiting to be dismissed.

What's got into him? the commander wondered, then shrugged it off. Dour was bringing in the rest of the away teams. Once everyone was there, he addressed the group, relaying the doctor's order. "I'd like everyone to prepare their reports and pass them to the bridge and to my quarters. No, wait."

He pointed to the engineering team. "You six. You're going to join me in auxiliary control. We'll isolate there."

The six who were chosen cheered and high-fived.

Lt. Doall spoke up, "Sir, do you want me there, too?"

"No, no. Let's have everyone pass their reports to you instead. I want to know what caused the space loonies on that ship, and when we have to go to prevent it from happening."

"Sir?"

"You'll understand if my idea works. Go on, all of you. Allons-y!"

Dour watched as everyone filed out. He turned to his mistress, the teleporter console, to reset the systems and run an analysis of whatever the decontamination process picked up, but the doors opened again, and one of the engineering minions came back in. She took a couple of steps toward him, opened her mouth to speak, then hesitated.

"Yes, Minion First Class? I have rituals to attend to."

"Oh, I know," she said. "I, uh, I wanted to thank you. You know, for, um, bringing us back in one piece and everything."

"I destroyed you and remade you in an image suiting to my Mistress's whims," he corrected. "It is my job."

She moved closer. "Yes, well, I just wanted to say you do a great job at it, and I appreciate it."

Then, with a sudden dash, she kissed him on the cheek and scurried away.

For a quick peck, it was certainly moist. He wiped his cheek with the back of his hand, then rubbed it against his pant leg. He thought no more of it. Teleporter chiefs were the masters of life and death on a daily basis. The bigger surprise was that they did not receive such adulation more often.

"They take us for granted, my Mistress," he murmured as he caressed the teleporter console. It seemed especially smooth under his fingertips.

* * *

Ellie Doall felt like there was something wrong with what had happened in the teleporter room, but she kept getting distracted by her teeth. She turned to her friend, Leslie, who was twirling the tricorders in one hand and sashaying with a little extra swing in her hips.

"Have you ever noticed how clean the decontamination leaves your teeth?" she asked her and ran her tongue along hers to show what she meant.

"Oh, I know! They're all smooth, like wet pearls!" Leslie ran her tongue over her own, but more slowly, savoring the feeling. A passing ensign glanced at her, then quickly looked away, embarrassed. She giggled.

Ellie sighed.

"Missing Hot Toddy?" Leslie asked.

"Always! I should be on Sapphire right now, getting to know his parents or maybe getting lost in those gorgeous blue eyes..."

"Or locking lips?" Leslie teased, then seeing her friend's frustrated, tortured expression, said, "Want to hit the gym?"

"Les! Isolation, remember? Besides, we have reports to compose."

"Reports, blah! Did you see how the LT dumped his homework on me? Hmmm..." She looked down the hall, saw a minion in Security Red, and yelled, "Tank! Come here!"

Minion Second Class Francisco "Tank" Martinez changed directions and went to them. "Lieutenants?"

Leslie passed him the tricorders. "These are the mission logs from the HMB Marvin. Go over them for anything unusual that might give a clue to what happened to the crew or that might pose a danger to the Impulsive. Flag them and send me the summary. Got it? Top priority. Preliminary report in 45 minutes. Good man."

She patted him on the cheek, then grabbed Ellie by the elbow and led her away before Tank could even get out a "Yes, ma'am."

"Leslie!" Ellie scolded. "Should you do that?"

"It's called 'delegation,' and every good leader knows to do it. You always do all the work yourself. If you ever want to be a First Officer on a bigger ship where you and Todd can be together all the time and make sweet, sweet love, you need to learn how to do it."

She sighed. "True...but not now. I need the distraction. Just saying his name gets me all hot and bothered."

Leslie laughed and wiped her brow. "It's not just that. It does seem hot in here. I guess we got used to the cold on the Marvin."

"I might turn down the temperature in my room for a bit. Anyway, this is my room. Now, go to your quarters until the doc calls, okay? I'm going to dig into space loonies and see what I can learn."

"Have fun." Leslie left her at her quarters and moved on. It was still the middle of the third shift, but mealtime, so there were more people in the hall than usual. Leslie smiled at them, thinking how lucky she was to be on a ship with so many great people—and attractive men.

And decontaminating teleporters, she thought, again running her tongue over her teeth. Nurse Bradshaw was passing by just then. He glanced at her, but unlike the other crewman, did not quickly turn away. Interesting.

What the hell, she thought, and strode up to him and kissed him soundly. Now he could quarantine with her, and that sounded a lot more fun.

* * *

Tank grunted as his superior officers sauntered away. He wondered casually what had gotten into the two ladies, but he wasn't the most curious person. His cheek itched, though, where Lt. Strauss had touched him. He wiped it with his hand, though how weird it was that her hands were so sweaty, then dismissed it. She gave him a task and a deadline.

He called in his new assignment to the duty officer, then went to a briefing room to view the files. The first one made him tilt his head in confusion. He squinted at the second one, not sure he believed what he was seeing. Before he finished the next one, however, he knew what he had to do.

"Tank to all available Security personnel. Meet me in Briefing Room 3—and bring beer."

He pulled off his shirt, revealing a black muscle shirt underneath, and set it over the back of the chair. Then he rewound the log he'd been watching, which showed several people running and ducking to avoid raser blasts while people cheered and placed bets. The guys were going to get a kick out of this.

* * *

The first thing Ellie did upon entering her quarters was to turn the temperature down five degrees. Then she downloaded the bridge logs into her computer and started to play them, but sitting in the chair made her think of the times she'd been sitting there with Todd reading over her shoulder, his breath tickling her ear. So, she set her computer on the floor so she could watch while standing on her head, but that made her think of how she tried to teach Todd that and she could hear his laugh. She flopped onto the couch, but that made her think of his kisses…

Fifty push-ups later, she lowered the temperature another degree, then tried again. This time, she noticed the message light blinking on her console. Her parents wanting, no doubt, to discuss her rash decision to fall in love with the perfect man…

"I can't concentrate here!" she yelled at the room. "Doall to Commander Smythe. Sir, can I *please* go work on the bridge?"

"Pardon? Yes, of course. Whatever you have to do. Just get me those spacetime coordinates."

"Spacetime…?"

"I trust you. We're a little busy right now. We need to reverse the polarity of the neutron flow." There was clanging and hammering in the background and something made a strained whooshing sound, then he clicked off.

What spacetime coordinates? That was weird. She shrugged it off. She was sure once she got to the bridge, she'd find exactly what he wanted. That was how it worked. After all, she was Lieutenant Ellie "Save the Ship" Doall.

And someday, she'd be Mrs. Lieutenant Ellie "Save the Ship" Doall Ahndmor!

What was I doing? she thought, then shrugged it off. She'd figure it out once she got to the bridge. She skipped out without grabbing her tricorder.

Second Officer's Log, Intergalactic Date 677001.335

We continue to maintain position relative to the HMB Marvin. (Pulsie, enter precise coordinates here, please.) The away teams have returned to the Impulsive and are self-isolating while...

Commander Richard Paolinelli paused in his log when the lazivator doors opened and Lieutenant Ellie Doall, Ops Officer, skipped out. "Lieutenant, why aren't you in quarters?"

"It's okay, sir. Commander Smythe said I could work up here."

"This is my shift!" Ensign Fyodor Smirnov protested.

Ellie pinched his cheek. "I won't bother you, Ensign Grumpypants. I'll take this console."

Grumpypants? "Paolinelli to Sickbay. Doctor, is Lieutenant Doall cleared for bridge duty?"

"Yes, it's fine," came the reply.

Little did Paolinelli know that the voice he heard was a simulation created by Commander Deary who was busy programming the doctor with a long-sleeved, frilly tunic and tight pants that ended at the ankles—the exact outfit Simone had worn in the last picture he had of her. Even so, the second officer wasn't sure their ops officer was fine, at all. "Lieutenant, a word?"

"Okee-dokee." She skipped down and sat primly in the first officer's seat. She looked at him with strained eyes, as if forcing herself to focus. She had a light sheen of sweat on her skin.

He set the back of his hand against her forehead. She didn't have a fever. "Are you sure you feel all right? You're sweating."

"Oh, it's probably because we had the Marvin at near freezing. But it's so sweet of you to notice."

He wasn't convinced. "Why don't you give me a preliminary report—your impressions, things we didn't get told over the comms?"

As she launched into her story, he scratched at the back of his hand. When she got to the part about the anvil, he was chuckling.

* * *

Ensign Daphne Becca was also looking at the logs she'd recorded, but she didn't find anything amusing about them.

That thing could have killed me, she thought as she watched the Marvin's doctor and nurse hauling up the anvil, giggling and bumping against each other like the boys back home did when they got into mischief.

She scowled at the image. *I did not join HuFleet and get my pilot training just so I could die on a stupid away mission because I think the captain is an attractive man.*

But he was so attractive…

She rubbed her clavicle (The bones below your neck! This is PG-13!), thinking about his chiseled jaw, his long legs. She did like them tall and lanky. How he was so confident and laid-back at the same time. Most of the people she'd grown up with were constantly uptight, always concerned about rules and decorum. Jebediah Tiberius was so different from them. Just how far did that difference go?

She left the log playing but opened a new file and typed out her letter of resignation. Then she went to change into something that would have gotten her The Pit on her homeworld. If she was going to quit HuFleet, she planned to go out in style.

* * *

The door chime woke Jeb from the first long sleep he'd been allowed since his concussion. Groggily, he rose, shoved his arms into his robe, and shuffled to the door, hand combing his hair into place.

"This had better be important," he started as the door slid open. The rest of what he was going to say got caught in his throat as he took in the beautiful woman in an elegant and revealing gown that stood before him.

"I resign my commission," she declared.

He squinted. Was he dreaming? Hallucinating? Had they entered an alternate dimension where he had replaced the evil version of himself? "Say again?"

She reached out and touched his bare chest. "Do you know where I was before I joined HuFleet, Captain?"

Her hand was warm, moist, and sent a curious shiver through him. He pushed his sleep-addled brain to find the answer to the question. "Gilead Four?"

"That's right. I was raised among the strictest society in the Union. I learned to milk cows and churn butter and never give a man a sideways glance but prepare myself to be seeded by whatever husband was chosen for me. I was eighteen when I escaped, but it's taken even longer to push past that indoctrination."

She stepped forward, her foot on the threshold.

"I think you're making great strides now," he said, and she giggled at his unintended pun. It was a very warm giggle. What had gotten into her?

She had both hands on his chest now, and it felt a little too right. He grabbed them but couldn't quite let go. "Ensign Becca, are you all right?"

"Daphne. And I'm righter than I've been in a long time. I know what I want. I want passion and joy, and to get my freak on all night and in the morning act like it never happened. From you, Captain. You're capable, aren't you?"

"Uh… Is this a mirror universe?"

"Would that help?"

He was starting to sweat, but he didn't even care. This had to be the mirror universe. He knew what he had to do.

He gave her a stern look. "My dear, I am a starship captain. I have been trained in multiple techniques, a broad variety of pleasuring."

"Oh, Jeb, you bad boy!"

She pushed him into his room. The doors closed on his "Yeehaw!"

* * *

Jeb was not the only one to be awakened from a sound sleep. Light years away, Todd Ahndmor, chief janbot programmer for CleanSpace Inc., yawned and rubbed the sleep out of his eyes before turning on his monitor. He rubbed them again as the bridge of the Impulsive appeared on the screen, Ellie in the first officer's seat, and some guy he didn't recognize sitting next to her and grinning like a schoolkid.

"Hi, Hot Toddy!" the bridge crew chorused.

"Um, hi? Ellie, what's going on?"

She sighed theatrically, "We're investigating this ship and all the people are dead and I just really, really missed you, so Rick said I could call you and say, 'Hi.' I love you!"

"I love you more," he replied automatically.

She responded, "I love you many stars," and the crew chorused, "awwww." Even the commander in the captain's chair looked more charmed than concerned. Was this some kind of prank?

He sat a little straighter. "Okay, seriously. What's going on? Where's the captain?"

The commander waved his hand vaguely. "He's in his quarters and doesn't want to be disturbed, and First Officer Phin is doing something in auxiliary control. But no worries. I'm in charge! I'll show you. Let's do a weapon's drill."

"Yes!" Ensign Sisco, who, being in charge of computer security, hardly ever got to shoot things, cheered. "Can I shoot up Marvin?"

"No!" the commander waggled his finger at him. "No. You do not get dessert first. Find me some debris and let's make it smaller."

"Marvin?" Todd yelped. "Who's Marvin?"

Ellie laughed, "The ship where everyone died, silly. That reminds me, I need to figure out some spacetime coordinates for Commander Phin. Do you know a language called Gallifreyan?"

Todd scanned the bridge. Sisco was punching buttons with two fingers and giggling. Smirnov was balancing between two consoles, his back on one, his feet on the other, frowning and half-dozing. He had his shirt off. In the back, two people were...kissing?

The commander started shouting out orders at random and people were calling out "Aye, aye!"

All of them looked like they were sweating.

"Ellie?" Todd said, "I think something is wrong."

"What?" She glanced around in annoyance. "I can't hear anything over these guys. Let's go to the Captain's Ready Room."

The bullpen team made catcalls and whistles as she stood, crooked her finger at the screen, and sashayed off the bridge. He'd never seen her move like that. In other circumstances, he'd have enjoyed it.

The screen changed as Ellie flopped herself onto the captain's couch. She kicked off her shoes and tucked her feet under her. She smiled at him, and there was so much love in her beautiful eyes, but they didn't seem completely focused.

"Ellie, did the people on the Marvin have some kind of infection?" he asked.

She toyed with her hair. "Maybe? It's space loonies, and no one knows what causes it. You should have seen how these people died. Some of them tried to jump across the warp core and a bunch crammed themselves into a lazivator—ooo! I have to log that. They broke the Union record!"

"Babe, how long does it take space loonies to spread?" As he asked, he searched for space loonies on his console. There wasn't a lot of information, mostly stories of ships found with the crew dead after having engaged in silly or inappropriate behavior.

"I don't know! That is a good point. I'm so glad Rickie let me call you. I'm going to work on that right now."

"What's Doc Sorcha say?"

"She hasn't said anything. First, she got squashed by an anvil!" Ellie broke into giggles. "Boom-smack! Commander Deary was going to fix her in Sickbay, and that's all I've heard since. She did say I was okay on the bridge. I mean, I think it was her. She did seem kind of odd."

"Maybe you should check on her?"

She huffed theatrically and lolled her head up to the ceiling. "Why? Don't you want to talk to me? I miss you so much."

She pulled off her shirt and leaned toward the screen. "So much," she repeated, her voice low and sultry.

He felt his pulse pounding. He cleared his throat. "I miss you, too, Ellie, but I'm worried. You're not acting like your normal self."

She reclined on the couch, striking a pose. She gave him a knowing smile. "You don't like how I'm acting?"

He coughed. "I do. I mean, I would, except you're lying on the captain's couch..."

"I am?" She blinked and looked around. Then, her eyes widened, and she sat up. "I am. Omigosh! I am! Todd, I have space loonies! I should be in quarantine. Oh, no!"

She leaped from the couch. He couldn't see what she was doing, but he heard the door open, then her squeal. When she flopped back onto the couch, she looked terrified. "Todd! They all have the loonies. I infected the bridge! Todd, I don't want to die. We have to get married first."

She started to look around wildly. "I have to get to Sapphire. I have to get to you."

"Honey! Breathe. I'm right here. We have to save the crew."

"But I want to marry you!"

He thought fast. "Me, too, but you want all your friends there, right? So, we have to find a way to cure everyone."

She paused, then smiled. "You're right! Omigosh, I almost forgot about that. Toddy, I'm not focusing very well. I thought coming to the bridge would help, but I made it all worse!"

"It's all right, my love. I'm here. I'm not going anywhere until we see this through. Don't hang up on me, okay?"

He hoped she didn't hear the fear in his voice, but something inside him said that if she cut the comms now, he'd never see her alive again.

*　*　*

Ellie and Todd weren't the only ones panicking. At that very moment, Ensign Gel O'Tin, the Impulsive's only gelatinous lifeform crewman, was slapping the door chime of his commander, Lt. LaFuentes, and begging, "Come on, LT. Open up, open up!"

Behind him, a couple was making their way down the hall by pressing each other against the walls in passionate kisses. Someone else was doing cartwheels. No one had paid Gel any attention except to laugh...other than Minion Leeta Umat, who had made a rather specific and inappropriate request. He'd managed to duck her by oozing through a vent, but now he heard her calling his name.

"Come on!" He was about to order a security override when the door finally opened, and Lieutenant LaFuentes leaned against the threshold. He wore only loose shorts. He had a raser in one hand and a mostly empty bottle in the other. Gel got the impression it wasn't his first.

"What?" LaFuentes demanded.

"Sir, the crew's gone insane!"

Enigo peered at the hallway and swore. "Am I the only one who knows what 'quarantine' means? Damn space loonies."

He shot from the hip and stunned the couple making out behind Gel. "You touched anybody this shift? No? Good. keep it that way."

"It's a contagion?" Gel asked. "It's spread crazy fast. I already contacted the bridge and they're all acting just as weird, and Commander Smythe is talking nonsense about time travel, and I can't get the captain to answer my calls and…. LT, we gotta do something!"

Enigo took a swig of his bottle, then belched. He scratched behind his ear with the butt of his raser. "No, I don't. I'm infected."

"But you're not acting…" He waved a pseudopod toward a shirtless crewman in tight pants brandishing a fencing foil and harrying other crewmen.

Enigo shot him, too.

He said, "That's 'cause I don't care, Ensign. I. Don't. Care."

"But Boss!"

"Loreli is gone, Gel! Dead, because I left her behind to save the fracking ship. That's how it always is. When do I get a break? It's been one crisis after another, and I gotta keep it together because I'm the goddamn Boss. Not this time. Loreli was the greatest love of my life, and I let her get killed! And don't give me that crap that she's still alive and everything will be okay. Even if the janbot was right, she's been with the Cybers. You think she'll be the same? She might be better off dead."

"LT..." Gel started, though he didn't know what he would say next. He'd seen his commander in a lot of moods, but never in such a combination of rage and grief. He looked at the bottle in his hand and wondered exactly what impulses he was trying to drown. He noticed the raser controls had been ripped off. To make sure he never took it off Stun?

"LT..."

Enigo cut him off. "I'm infected. Compromised. I don't care about nothing. You don't want me out there. Time to shine, Ensign."

Down the hall, someone was cooing Gel's name and inviting him to take a bath, with him as the bath. Umat had caught up to him. Gel quivered with anxiety.

"But I'm just an ensign. I can't—I mean, literally!"

"Yeah. Good point." He scratched his head with the butt of the raser while he thought. "Pulsie! Transfer all Chief of Security command privileges to Ensign Gel O'Tin. Authorization LaFuentes, Enigo." Enigo then rattled off a security code the universal translator covered in static.

The computerized voice of the HMB Impulsive said, "Done."

"There. Now you can do anything I can. Make us proud."

"What if I can't?"

He shrugged. "Then we all die, but I'll be with Loreli. That's a win for me."

Enigo brought the bottle to his lips, found it empty, and with a snarl, hurled it against the wall. Since breakable glass was not a great idea on a starship, the bottle did not shatter but left a dent in the wall.

He retreated back to his quarters.

"Gel," a voice sing-songed from around the corner. "Come wrap that sexy viscous body of yours all over me."

With a swear word that the translator didn't translate, he oozed into the nearest vent.

He didn't stop until he was five decks up and three sections over. Then, he settled into a corner and allowed himself exactly ten seconds of panicked shivering before forcing his mind to the situation.

There was nothing in the security manual about space loonies, or about shipwide contagions. Those were under the responsibility of Medical, and Security just followed orders. He'd already tried to contact Sickbay, but no one answered, and Pulsie said the EMPT was offline.

Okay, so what would Sickbay do? The LT said something about a quarantine. "Pulsie, send out a distress beacon with the applicable ship logs. Then, I want you to lock all quarters, Security authorization O'Tin, Gel..." He blopped out his code in his native language.

"You got it," the ship replied.

What next? He'd left his quarters to go to the gym and found the ship in chaos. Other than what Lt. LaFuentes had told him and what he'd seen with his own receptors, he had no idea what was going on.

If this is a disease and not an invasion, we need the holodoc. He started toward Sickbay, grateful for all the training they'd done wandering the vents and Jeffries tubes. It was a little chillier, but he'd move more easily without having to dodge infected crewmen—or Minion Umat. In the meantime, he asked Pulsie to give him a quick summary of what had happened since he went off duty.

As the news went from horrifying to dismal, Gel felt his panic growing. "Pulsie, stop! Can you tell who's been infected and who hasn't?"

"Hang on… Well, the surest way would be to track vectors starting with anyone who's touched the away team members. That's going to take a while, and a lot of my processing power is being diverted by auxiliary control for the TARDIS."

"The what? Never mind." He couldn't override the Impulsive's First Officer, anyway. He got to the junction just before Sickbay and took the left. He heard music from that direction, but not the wilder stuff he'd heard several times already. This was calmer, more romantic. "What about a common symptom? Other than stupidity, I mean."

"Well, most people seem to be running a low-grade fever, though they're sweating a lot more. More like hot flashes, only longer-lasting."

He heard a warm laugh. It almost sounded like Doc Sorcha.

"Okay, let's look for that. Start with any medical personnel trapped in their rooms. I gotta go silent while I assess the situation in Sickbay."

"You got it!" Pulsie agreed.

Gel edged to the vent and peeked into Sickbay, which was dark. No, not dark. Dim. The lights were off, but there were holographic candles floating near the ceiling and along the walls. The romantic music was coming from this room.

In the center of the medical bay, Commander Deary was dancing with Doc Sorcha, only it wasn't the holodoc. Her figure had been altered, and she looked about ten years younger, and she wore a slinky evening gown.

Was she in her role as Ship's Sexy? He dismissed the idea. She'd have dropped the facade as soon as he'd called her for help. Pulsie had said the program was offline, anyway.

The commander gazed at her and sighed, "Ah, Simone, where did we go wrong?"

She pressed her fingers against his lips. "It doesn't matter. We're together now."

While the two kissed, Gel backed up and told Pulsie to extend his search for programmers as well.

"Ellie to Gel!" Lieutenant Doall's cheery voice cut across the response of the Impulsive. "Gel, you awake?"

* * *

"Lieutenant Ellie DoItAll to Gel the Goopy! Wakey, wakey!"

"Lieutenant!" Gel almost gushed with relief, then he realized what she'd just said. "You're infected, aren't you?"

She responded with a giggle and hum of pleasure. "Of course, silly! Are you?"

"No. Lieutenant, can you—"

"Ellie. You can call me Ellie, you know. I like my name. I like it even better when Todd says it. Oh! Oh! Someone wants to say, 'hi.'"

The voice of Todd Ahndmor, her fiancé, said, "Hey, Gel. I'm so glad you're not infected."

Wasn't he? Maybe he was hallucinating. "Uh, Todd? Where are you?"

"Don't worry, I'm safe on Sapphire. Ellie called me."

"I missed him so much!" she cut in. "He said he'd help me with our project."

"What project?"

She laughed. "Saving the ship, of course! Just don't make me do it myself this time. I hate doing group projects all by myself. When I was in school, the girls always left the work to me. 'Oh, do be a dear, Ellie. I have important princess things to do...'" Her voice turned haughty and sneering.

Todd cut in, "You're my princess, Ellibean, and we're not leaving this to you alone. Right, Gel?"

While she giggled and cooed, "Princess Ellibean and Prince Toddybear!" Todd said in a private channel, "Gel? How much do you know about what's going on?"

"Maybe as much as you," he replied. "Is she okay?"

"I'm trying to keep her focused on the problem, but she'd rather talk about uh...other things."

"That seems to be a running theme." He'd been making himself ignore the sloppy sounds coming through the vents, except where they might indicate someone was moving through the vents, like Umat.

"I'll bet. Anyway. I'm not leaving until you guys are safe, okay? Whatever I can do from here, I will."

"Hey!" Ellie cut in, her voice suddenly afraid. "Are you still there?"

"Yes, Lieutenant," Gel said.

"Always," Todd said. "How about we start with what we've each done? Ell locked down all the airlocks, the shuttle doors, and the weapons lockers. We're going through the logs to try and get ahead of any other dangerously stupid stunts this thing makes people do."

"It's kind of fun!" Ellie said. "What have you been doing?"

She applauded as Gel gave her his status. "You are so smart, Gel! I totally should have thought of a distress call. I'll be so happy to see rescue, I could hug them all!"

Todd said, "Gel, did that distress call say anything about wearing protective gear?"

The Impulsive computer cut in. "I marked us as a Class One Biohazard."

Ellie made a distressed sound. "Oh! Right. We don't want to spread this. I'm sorry. I just want to hug someone—you, Toddybear—and kiss you and… Oh! And it's so hot in here!"

"Really?" Gel said. "I'm chilly."

Todd said, "Concentrate, guys. We're on the clock. According to the reports and the logs, the crew of the Marvin went from silly to suicidally stupid in about five hours. Ellie said they got back to the Impulsive about two hours ago."

"Do you know what caused it? Or better yet, how we can cure it?"

"There's nothing in the records we found."

Gel shivered. "First priority is to get the holodoc back online."

"Can you figure that out?" Ellie asked, her tone lazy. "I have to talk to Todd. Privately."

Todd's voice was playful and scolding. "Princess, we agreed. First work, then play. I promise it will be worth it."

"Oooh! Do tell."

"Oh, no," Todd teased. "You have to earn it. How do you get the holodoc online?"

While Todd worked to get Ellie back on task, Gel muted the line and told the Impulsive to flood Lt. LaFuentes' room with knock-out gas and keep him unconscious until all this was over. He'd never forgive himself if he let the Boss get stupidly suicidal.

Meanwhile, Ellie said, "Okay, okay… Um… We're sure she's offline?"

Gel said, "He's calling her 'Simone,' and they're making out. I don't think that's in the Doc's personality."

"Aww," Ellie cooed. "That's his old girlfriend. He must be lonely. I'm so glad I have you, Toddybear."

Todd said, "Did he overlay a personality, then? Ellibean, can you override it?"

"Assuming she was already compromised when I came on the bridge, he'd have had 20 minutes to make the changes. That's not enough time for a full overhaul. He probably used a cascading overlay across descending matrices using the real Simone's personality files and any memorabilia."

"You're so hot when you talk tech," Todd sighed, and Gel didn't think he'd said it just to encourage her.

"What do we do?" Gel demanded.

Ellie continued. "It's probably overwriting the code we instituted as new behaviors are introduced. The longer we delay, the longer the program runs, the more extensive the revisions. The EMPT can only be modified in Sickbay by someone with a Class Three Computer Operations Clearance and permission from ops. I can give the permissions. So, Class Three... Commander Paolinelli and Ensign Sisco are infected. Chief Lewis?"

"Infected," Pulsie said, "and Senior Minion Lassiter."

"Well, that's bad," Ellie said, then hummed. "Have you ever noticed how soft the captain's couch is?"

Gel cringed and added this to the list of things he vowed to forget when this was all over. "LT? Can we just reboot her? If we powered her down, could we restart with the backup?"

"Yes! Then we need to get Tank to download the Marvin's sickbay files. Leslie delegated to him. I hope Leslie's okay. You know, she likes how decontamination makes your teeth feel, too. Okay, umm... What are we looking for?"

"To power down the doc!" both Gel and Todd answered.

"Right. Sorry. This'll be fun. So, you know the main medical programming console, right?

Where we plug in the portadoc when it's not been squashed by an anvil? There's a panel on the lower front..."

* * *

Gel had stiffened up in the cold of the vents; a normal thing for a human, but not for a Globbal. He moved more slowly than normal and found he had to repeat Ellie's instructions to keep them in his mind. While he rebooted the holodoc, she was going to try to find and load the Marvin's medical records and find a way to get their infected crewmates into a common area. He paused at the vent and sent out one tentacle to look around.

Commander Deary had darkened most of Sickbay and used the holographic generators to create a fire in a fireplace and a large couch in the far corner. He and "Simone" were sitting in it, kissing. Well, he assumed from the sloppy meat smacking sounds and hums that they were kissing; other than an occasional flash of the top of one's head, he couldn't see them.

No point trying to stun the Commander, then. He couldn't get a clear shot from the vent, and the raser would not fit through the slats in the vent cover. He'd have to disable the doc, then take out their chief engineer if needed.

That would make the second senior officer I've taken out in the space of an hour. I wonder if I'll get a commendation or a reprimand?

He carefully oozed out into Sickbay, keeping to the edge of the floor, trying to stay in the shadows. It was a degree or two warmer in the room, and relief washed over him as the fluids of his body again loosened up. He moved slowly, nonetheless, pausing when he heard a rustle from the couch. Naturally, the vent he'd exited was across the room from his target.

Suddenly, Elie's voice sounded over the intercom. "Attention, everybody! Pizza Party in the mess hall!"

"What was that?" Simone yelped and sat up, scanning the room. She saw Gel and screeched.

Cover blown, Gel raced to the Sickbay controls.

Suddenly, Simone was there. She swung to slap Gel away, but instead of a human hand that he would have easily flowed around, he was instead struck by a forcefield that flung him back hard against the wall. His body, still not fully thawed, did not absorb the blow with its usual alacrity. The world grayed around him for a moment.

Simone was on him, screaming and smacking him. Commander Deary was shouting for her to stop as he tried to scramble over the couch. His foot caught on the back, and he fell flat on his face. Over the intercom, Ellie was going on about birthdays and cake.

There was a small intake vent near Gel. He chose the better part of valor and oozed into it as fast as he could. He heard a metallic twang as she kicked the vent. Then he heard the commander yelling and her yelling back.

He kept moving.

He took the first left, then paused to assess his injuries. He had been hurt, but fortunately, not as badly as he'd expected. Even so, it kind of unnerved him. "O'Tin to Doall."

"Gel! Hi! And call me, 'Ellie.' Did you hear about the party? That should get everyone to the mess hall, where we can lock them in. Oh, but I did program the replicators to make pizza and cake and ice cream and..."

"Ellie! I failed. I couldn't get to the Sickbay controls. The doc may think she's the commander's old flame, but she still moves like a photonic being. She kicked my butt. Is there another way to reboot the system? A failsafe or something?"

But Ellie was still going on about cake.

"Todd? Todd, are you still there?"

Ellie replied, "Oh, he's offline for just a minute. He's calling off work, for a 'family emergency.' Isn't it sweet? We're his family! Oh, Gel, I love him so much. He's so sweet and wikadas smart and sexy…"

The Ship is Family, Gel thought. That was the first thing Lieutenant LaFuentes had taught them. The second thing—well, the second thing was "When in doubt, stun them all," but the third thing was "Always have a backup plan."

The Boss would know the holodoc could be compromised. How would he plan for that contingency?

"Pulsie," Gel called out, grateful that the ship's AI was not subject to the virus. "Is there any way the Chief of Security can reboot the holodoc?"

"As a matter of fact, Acting Chief, there's a switch in the security office."

Gel groaned. Sickbay was in the Saucer Section. Security was in the Other Section—five levels and 500 meters away. Ellie's nattering was starting to blur into a buzzing. He was so sore. Maybe he could take a minute...

Something clanged against the vent, and the shouting between Commander Deary and his holographic girlfriend got louder. Gel heaved himself toward the security office and the reset button. Regardless of what happened with Doc Sorcha, he was going to get rid of Simone.

* * *

"Gel?" Todd's voice came over the intercom in the stilted way that told Gel he was typing the message. "Did you reset the holodoc?"

"I'm working on it," Gel snapped. He was one level away from the security office, but every inch was harder than the one before. Only another hundred meters...

"Okay, but you need to hurry. Ellie's getting worse. It's getting harder to keep her focused. I mean, she's focused, but it's only on—"

"I don't want to know!"

"You okay? Oh, no, Gel! You're not infected, too?"

"No, I'm just freezing."

"Really? She keeps saying it's too hot. In fact, she's still sweating, and she's removed most of her uniform."

"She's human, Todd. I'm a Globbal, remember? The temperature's been turned way down, and I don't have the authority to override it. Wait! The LT can. Make her turn it up."

"How?" Todd's voice rang with frustration bordering on panic. "I'm running out of ideas! Now, she's obsessed with joining the pizza party. It's getting hard to even keep her in the ready room, much less saving the ship. And I'm dead serious that she doesn't have much on. Does that sound like her? Come on, Gel. You've known her much longer than I have. What motivates her?"

Why do I have to do everything? he thought. At least getting mad was taking his mind off the pain. "Tell her Lieutenant LaFuentes will break your face if she doesn't save the ship."

"Good one! I'm on it. Hey, has Ellie been hitting the gym more lately? Because she's really, really..."

"I don't want to know!"

* * *

Gel didn't so much slip as plop his way out of the vent and into Lt. LaFuentes' office. Never in his life had he felt so heavy and solid. It was a couple of degrees warmer than in the vents, where cool air continued to circulate despite Todd's best efforts to get Ellie to turn up the heat. Someone in Environmental Control had set the controls to "Down," and disabled them. The best Ellie had been able to do was set a lower limit; unfortunately, it was lower than Gel's lowest tolerance.

He paused on the floor, taking in the relative warmth. If he'd had lungs, he would have breathed a sigh of relief. Then, imagining the LT yelling at him to stop being a babimann, he struggled to the workstation and heaved himself onto the chair since he no longer had the flexibility to stretch high enough to reach the panel. Pulsie had told him that first, he had to activate the controls, then he had to physically flip the switch. Gel grumbled under his breath about unnecessary plot complications.

His cytoplasm was thick and cold; it took several tries to tap in the sequence. At last, the computer acknowledged his access.

Globbals didn't "see" in the same way humans did, but suffice to say things were getting blurry and hard to define. His outer layer was growing numb, too. It took several minutes to find the switch and throw it. He counted slowly to ten and flipped it again.

Another ten-count, and he called, "Gel to Doc Sorcha..."

The familiar, acerbic voice of their holodoc responded, "We need to have a conversation about access to my controls. I've lost almost an hour and fifteen minutes, and I've just had to sedate Commander Deary. Who is Simone?"

"Never mind. We have about 45 minutes for you to figure out how to cure everyone. Upload the file DoallDoesDiseases and please don't ask me why it's named that. Most of the crew is locked in the mess. I'm releasing the uninfected crewmen now." He gave the security command.

"Ensign? Your body temperature is fifteen degrees below normal. You cannot maintain that level of chill."

Gel laughed. The rest of what the doc said faded into the background.

"Gel?" Ellie's voice cut through his mental fog. "Gel! Wake up."

"Ellie? Are you cured?" He forced himself to concentrate. He slouched in a malformed blob near the holodoc's reset switch. He'd tripped it, right?

Ellie squealed with delight. "You called me, 'Ellie!' I've missed that. You're always so formal now that I outrank you again. But you did it. Doc Sorcha is online and cranky as ever! But we're worried about you. You have to get someplace warm. Go to the Botany lab. It's on an independent system."

The botany lab was back in the Saucer Section. Gel laughed weakly.

But Ellie didn't laugh with him. "It's not funny this time! You have to get warm. Go, quick."

"Everything's blurry."

"You can't die on me, Gel!" she said, then her voice grew hard. "Move—that's an order!"

His body felt thick, heavy, and solid. It ached in ways he never knew existed. But the lieutenant continued to yell and cajole, and Todd added his voice. Gel gathered up his energy and moved.

Normally, Gel flowed, the fluid that made up his being drifting and surging in the direction he needed to go. Now, each movement was a game of push and pull, of shoving the iciest part of himself forward, the warmer, more flexible parts of his being swirling around, then pushing and pulling again. Every bit of progress came with the pain of impact he could not absorb. Everything seemed dark and weird and cold, and he clung to Ellie's voice like a lifeline, turning when she told him to, pushing forward while she cried that he couldn't die like Loreli...

Then came the moment when he tried to shove himself forward, and his body could not move.

"LT? Ellie? I'm...stuck... Too cold..."

"No, you have to!" she begged, then he heard her muttering. "Come on, Ellie, think! This can't happen again!" Then she fell to sobbing.

"It's okay," he murmured, but he didn't know if she heard him. Todd was consoling her, trying to get her back on task, telling her to imagine him there with her, his arms around her, snuggling as they worked out the problem...

Great. The last thing he'd hear before dying was human sexy talk.

"I don't want to know..." he muttered to himself and laughed.

Suddenly, she shouted, "That's it!"

A moment later, over the intercom, he heard her voice. "Attention Deck Five, Section C. Ensign Gel needs hugs! Let's snuggle our favorite Globbal!"

"Wha...?"

People in various stages of dress came running from seeming nowhere and everywhere, arms outstretched and yelling, "Hug him! Hug him!"

I hope Umat isn't in this section, he thought as crewmen started to pile on him.

* * *

Captain's Log, Intergalactic Date 677001.38

Despite having been offline for most of the crisis, Doc Sorcha came back in true form, literally and figuratively, and was able to determine the correct amount of imposazine to cure everyone of the space loonies. It would not have been possible, however, without the work of Lieutenant Ellie Doall and the heroic efforts of Ensign Gel O'Tin, who is in Sickbay recovering from near-fatal hypothermia.

Unfortunately, while under the influence, the bridge night watch B Team used the HMB

Marvin for target practice, which set off something called the Illudium Pew-36. The ship was vaporized, and the debris sucked into the gravitational pull of the collapsing star. It's a tragic loss, and yet fitting when considering how other ships affected by the space loonies have met their demise.

On the Impulsive, we've got a lot of repairs to do, not only to the ship, but to relationships and, for some, our own vision of ourselves. I expect things will be awkward for a while, but if any crew can work through chaos of their own design, it's my people.

Gel woke up feeling viscous and blissfully warm, contained in a tank in Sickbay with heat lamps shining on him and the humidity turned high. He sighed, slopping waves against the sides of the tank, reveling in his fluidity.

"'Bout time, hero," Lt. LaFuentes said. He stood from his chair to smile at Gel. The Boss was flushed and sweating.

Gel drew back. "Are you still infected, sir?"

"Nah, blame your treatment!" He indicated the heat lamps. "Doc Sorcha cured us all. There were some injuries, mucho embarrassment, and I dunno what happened in auxiliary control, but no one died. Thanks to you."

Gel blushed with pride, which is to say, he turned a slight teal. "Not just me, sir. Lieutenant Doall—and Todd Ahndmor. In fact, I think if it weren't for Todd, we might not have made it. He kept the LT on task, and she was *really* affected."

"Yeah, I know. Before the cure got to her, she was supervising your rescue wrapped up in the captain's Texas flag."

He thought he remembered a glimpse of a white star surrounded in blue before the bodies piled onto him. "I'm kind of glad I was out for all of that."

"Yeah, I heard it got a little surreal. 'Course I wouldn't know because someone gassed me in my own room."

Now, Gel blushed for a different reason. "Sorry, sir. It's just they said some people killed themselves on the Marvin…"

"I ain't suicidal. Ever. Got it? Still, I appreciate the sentiment, and it was a gutsy move. You done us proud, Ensign. So, you're probably gonna get a medal, and I thought I should warn you. I mean, thrilling heroics, enduring extreme psychological and environmental stresses... Your homeworld will probably want you to come back and mate again."

"Aw..."

* * *

Captain Jeb Tiberius stood in the entryway of Auxiliary Control, hands on his hips and mouth open so wide his momma would have accused him of catching flies.

The room had been completely transformed. The long consoles that arched across the back of the room in a replica of the bridge had been moved to form a hexagon around a large tube that stretched from floor to ceiling. Casings bearing odd, circular script covered the top. They spun as the glow inside the casing moved up and down.

His first officer and best friend stood beside the part of the console that also contained what looked like a bronze laptop and a waffle iron. He wore a fez and carried the weird device he'd found on Rest Stop. He was doing his best to look dignified and not like he'd rather run out an airlock and join the UFS Marvin on its way to doom. In the back of the room, six junior engineers looked ashamed, baffled, yet somehow accomplished.

How had they managed to do so much in three hours?

Jeb found control of his jaw muscles and spoke. "Please tell me that's not antimatter in that glowy chamber."

Smythe remained silent. The engineering team shifted their feet and looked at each other or the floor.

"I... see. If we mess with that twirly thing, will it send us back in time?" He pointed at the eggbeater.

"No, Captain," Smythe replied.

"We hadn't connected it yet," one of the engineers added and was elbowed by both men beside him.

Jeb looked toward the ceiling. "Captain to Engineering. Are we warp-capable?"

"Engineer's Mate Minion Dionysus, sir. Not yet, sir, but maybe thirty minutes?" came the reply. In the background, they heard Commander Deary screaming abuses, bemoaning his "wee bairns," yelling about glitter, and vowing something about a devil woman distracting him for the last time.

"Thank you, Dionysus. Captain out." Jeb looked at the engineering team before him. "All things considered, y'all might be better off fixing this mess. Commander, if you would...?"

Smythe started to follow. Before he got to the door, he paused, pulled off the fez, and placed it on the console. He kept the sonic screwdriver, however.

Once in the hall, he said, "Jeb, I'm mortified. I have no idea how we got so out of control."

Jeb held up his hand to stop further explanation. "No one infected was responsible for their actions. Let's just make things right."

Ensign Becca passed by them in the hall. She and Jeb glanced at each other, then quickly away. Daphne'd already told him she was sincere about resigning, but it was still going to be an awkward couple of weeks until they could drop her off at a starbase.

In the meantime, he had his own amends to make to a certain captain who also had command of his heart. Even with the extenuating circumstances considered, she deserved an explanation, and it was best to be proactive.

Jeb turned back to his friend. "Remind me again what goes into an apology bouquet."

Smythe glanced at the retreating ensign, though he kept his expression impassive. "Oh, dear."

"Ah-yep."

"White tulips, purple hyacinth, daffodils…" He rattled off the list known from years of watching his father apologize to his mother.

When they got to the bridge, Jeb left Commander Smythe the conn while he went to his ready room. No sense putting it off.

He stopped short to find Lieutenant Doall polishing his furniture. "Lieutenant?"

She yelped in surprise and snatched the cloths from the couch, wrapping them into a ball.

"Um, welcome back, Captain!" she said and dashed out of the room.

"It's good to be back," he told the empty room, bemused, then, with a sigh, sat at his desk to send the replicator order to Kat and to call with his apologies. He caught sight of his wall and frowned.

Was his flag crooked?

There are more adventures to come!

Get the next Space Traipse right now on Amazon!

Thanks for Reading!

I'd like to thank the beta readers who so generously gave their time to seek out my typos: Deborah Cullins Smith, Jane Lebak, Karrie Lapoehn, Steven R. McEvoy, Also, a shout out to Kalonda Coleman, a new editor on the scene, who decided to cut her teeth on my manuscript.

2020 was an insane year, and the best and worst year to publish my silly adventures. Worst because...2020. People had a lot on their minds. Best because I was able to make some folks laugh in a year that strove to make us all weep. It makes me feel good to know that I provided a small respite. Now, we're in 2021. I pray the year shows a recovering world, not just economically, but in optimism and hope. That is our future. That's the attitude I bring to every Space Traipse story. May it be contagious.

Because I'd rather we not have an Armageddon-level war to bring about warp drive. Who wants to be motivated by that kind of negativity? How much better to think, "Warp drive? Sure. Hold my beer!"

Thanks again for joining me in my fun.

About the Author

Karina Fabian lives on Ground Zero for potential Xindi attack, but she can watch rocket launches from her front yard, so that's a plus. In 1990, she married a steely-eyed spaceman, Rob, who is now the President of Vaya Space. She writes fictional space travel while he works to make it true. In the meantime, they raised four great kids.

Keep in Touch

If you want to learn about future books, please
- Sign up for my newsletter. https://fabianspace.substack.com/subscribe for more stories, updates and a free book!
- Visit my website (https://karinafabian.com)
- Follow me on Facebook: https://www.facebook.com/Karina-Fabian-Speculative-Fiction-with-a-Grin-2233839790277963
- Join HuFleet—follow the Impulsive on Facebook: https://www.facebook.com/sthmb/

There's More Fun in FabianSpace!

Thank you for buying this book. If you enjoyed it, click to see the others in this series or discover one of the other worlds of FabianSpace.

Science Fiction
Space Traipse: Hold My Beer: Redneck ingenuity and common sense in a Star Trek-ish universe. Enjoy the adventures of the HMB Impulsive.
The Rescue Sisters: Intrepid women doing dangerous missions in space for the love of God and humankind.
The Old Man and the Void: Dex is a relic hunter on the edge of the black hole, desperate for the catch of a lifetime.
Jovian Heat: As the next Great Storm of Jupiter rises, Cass must find the father of a baby in peril—but the father died before the child was conceived.

Fantasy
DragonEye: Vern's a snarky dragon on the wrong side of the Interdimensional Gap, solving crimes, battling evil, and saving the universes on an all-too-regular basis.
Madness of Kanaan: Deryl isn't crazy; he's psychic, and aliens of two worlds thinks he can save them. Maybe he can—but can he regain his sanity in the process?

Horror
Neeta Lyffe, Zombie Exterminator: Neeta's an average exterminator, taking out bugs, rodents, and the undead. Can she keep her friends alive, pay her bills, and find romance?
Frightliner and Other Tales of the Supernatural (with Colleen Drippé): Truck-driving vampires terrorizing the road, Southern women doing what needs doing, a zombie wedding—a great story collection for horror lovers.